PROTÉGÉ OF A LEGEND 3

Corey Robinson

**Lock Down Publications and Ca$h
Presents**
Protégé of a Legend 3
A Novel by *Corey Robinson*

Protege of a Legend 3

Lock Down Publications
Po Box 944
Stockbridge, Ga 30281

Visit our website @
www.lockdownpublications.com

Lock Down Publications
Like our page on Facebook: Lock Down Publications @
www.facebook.com/lockdownpublications.ldp
Book interior design by: **Shawn Walker**

Corey Robinson

Stay Connected with Us!

Text **LOCKDOWN** to 22828 to stay up-to-date with new releases, sneak peaks, contests and more...
Thank you.

Submission Guideline.

Submit the first three chapters of your completed manuscript to ldpsubmissions@gmail.com, subject line: Your book's title. The manuscript must be in a .doc file and sent as an attachment. Document should be in Times New Roman, double spaced and in size 12 font. Also, provide your synopsis and full contact information. If sending multiple submissions, they must each be in a separate email.

Have a story but no way to send it electronically? You can still submit to LDP/Ca$h Presents. Send in the first three chapters, written or typed, of your completed manuscript to:

LDP: Submissions Dept
Po Box 944
Stockbridge, Ga 30281

DO NOT send original manuscript. Must be a duplicate.

Provide your synopsis and a cover letter containing your full contact information.

Thanks for considering LDP and Ca$h Presents.

Corey Robinson

Prologue

"Madison, let's go. I hope you got your shit packed because it's time for you to get out of here," the prison guard hollered. When I heard my name called I dragged myself out of the bed I had slept in for ten years of my life, although, deep inside, I wasn't ready. I had become accustomed to my circumstances and was in no rush to leave.

"Madison, get your shit together now," she yelled again and when my cell door opened, I looked up at her with fear in my eyes. I slowly gathered what little bit of belongings I had accumulated over the years. I didn't understand how the system could put me out knowing that I had no place to go. That cell had been my life for a while and I had learned to accept it as my home.

I asked the guard, "do you really have to rush me?" She laughed but I didn't find shit funny. I was dead ass serious. She replied, "ya know Madison, I've worked here for a long time and I have never heard anyone ask a question like that. Most inmates don't even give me a chance to call for them. They actually come looking for me so they can get the hell outta here," She looked at me with a concerned look in her eyes and stated, "I know you might be a little nervous after being gone for so long but you are still young and still have so much life to live. Go out there and enjoy yourself."

"Yeah, you can say shit like that because when you walk out of here, you have a place to call home. I don't have shit," I said and grabbed my small bag. When I stopped out of the cell, I bumped into the guard and said, "fuck it, I'm outta here."

The guard called my name and when I turned around, she asked, "what are your plans?"

I looked at her through heartless eyes and said, "I'm about to make a motherfucker feel my pain," and then I walked away and prepared my mind to face the bastard who'd left me for dead.

Corey Robinson

Chapter One

"Pow Pow Pow," Khalif said anxiously when he held the gun out in front of him and although it was only a toy, it bothered me just the same.

"Khalif, put that damn toy gun away. Can't you find something else to play with?" I exclaimed while I looked at him through concerned eyes.

Khalif had turned eleven years old only a few weeks ago and his uncle Marcus had gifted him with the piece he held in his hand. I wasn't happy about it because I didn't want my son to have the kind of life his father had lived. I tried hard to shield him from the streets but every time I looked into his saddened eyes, I could see the block. I knew that he had been born with the hustler mentality and even though he had never met his father, he idolized him just the same.

"Uncle Marcus said that my dad had a perfect aim and I'm gonna be just like him. Pow Pow Pow," Khalif shouted out and pointed the gun at me with a familiar glint in his eyes, one that scared the hell out of me. I stood frozen for a minute and looked at Feelow's replica; my heart still broke from his death. To everyone who knew him, he wasn't always the greatest but to the child who stood in front of me and pointed a gun, he was an immortal luminary and no one could tell him different.

"Son, put that damn gun away and find something else to play with or I'm going to take it. Do you understand me?" I stated sternly so that he would understand that I was not playing.

"Ah ma, I ain't hurtin' nobody. I'm just trying to get my aim on point. I got to prepare myself," he said and put the gun in the waist of his jeans that he had dropped to the middle of his ass like a street thug. He sat down on the end of his bed and crossed his arms over his chest and pouted. I breathed in a heavy sigh of relief and before I turned away to walk out of his room I said, "and pull those damn pants up. I'm not raising a street thug. Dammit Khalif, you are going to be somebody when you grow up even if I have to beat it into you."

Khalif replied before I shut the bedroom door, "you damn right, I'm gonna be somebody, I'm gonna be my daddy."

I shut the door and stood with my back against it and thought about what he'd said, "I got to prepare myself." I wasn't sure just what he'd meant by that comment, so I opened the door back up and asked him, "Khalif, what did you mean by that comment you made about preparing yourself? What the hell are you talking about?"

He stood up from the corner of the bed he had sat on and walked over to his dresser. He pulled out his bottom drawer and reached his small hand inside. He then took a picture out from under the clothes his drawer possessed and stared at it for a second before he answered my question, "I'm preparing myself so that I don't miss when I shoot that bitch who took my daddy from me." The chills shot down my spine instantly because I could feel the seriousness in his tone.

I walked over to him and pulled the picture from his hand and looked into the eyes of the woman who confessed to eliminating Feelow from the earth. I pulled my son into my embrace and said in a soft motherly voice, "no son. If you do, that would make you no better than her. She has paid for what she did, so let's move on."

Khalif pulled away from me and snatched the photo back from me. He then said through soulless eyes, "nah ma, she still owes me and I want that debt cleared. I'm a send that white bitch to hell," and then he ran quickly out of the room. I jumped when I heard the front door slam and knew that there was nothing I could do to change his mind. My eleven-year-old son had murder consuming his thoughts and was possessed by the spirit of his father.

"Damn you Feelow. I fucking need you right now. Why in the hell didn't you fight? Damn it," I stated out loud and somehow felt like Feelow could hear me. I sat on the side of Khalif's bed and crossed my arms over my chest to bring myself some comfort. I wanted to send a prayer up for my child but wondered if God would even listen. I noticed a notebook sticking out from under my son's pillow and pulled it out. I opened it and saw clippings from the story of Feelow murder pasted on to the pages. I wondered just how long my child had plotted to murder the girl on the paper and then I saw Marcus' face. I couldn't believe that they had actually thought he would kill his best friend. They claimed an eyewitness had reportedly seen Marcus do it but no one ever took the stand against him. The state still tried to convict him because they didn't care about sending a black man away. However, Marcus was spared, thanks to the white girl admitting to the sin she had committed. My mind had always wondered if she was really the culprit but I just brushed it off. A thought suddenly entered my mind, "oh my God, it's time." I stated out loud and then replaced the notebook where I got it from. I jumped up and ran out of the room so I could hit the streets and find my son, the only piece of Feelow I had left.

***

"Your pops is gonna make you the king of the streets one day, shit, you gonna be bigger than I ever was," I said to Markill, my ten-year-old son. He would turn eleven in another month. I had planned on gifting him a nine-millimeter pellet gun for his birthday. The same kind I had given Khalif when he turned eleven. Keisha wasn't happy with Khalif's gift but he was my best friend's seed and my nephew. I wanted that lil' nigga and my son to start out young. The streets were crucial to a black child, especially a male; they needed to know just how shit worked.

I was lost in thought when I heard the sweetest voice I'd ever known, "Marcus, I have to go. I'm supposed to be meeting up with a potential investor and if I get the contract, it could mean a promotion for me," Killisha said with a smile on her beautiful face. I had met Killisha a little over a year before I got recruited into the dope game. I didn't have shit, not even a place to call home but she saw something in me no one else did. I had kept her tucked away from my life in the streets because I didn't want any harm to come to her.

She was a good girl who had graduated high school and went on to college. She now worked for a high-end investment firm and made good money. She had been pregnant with Markill when I was going through a trial for Feelow's murder. If it hadn't been for Krystal, the white bitch I was fucking on the side, I wouldn't have been enjoying a life full of freedom. That dumb bitch took the charge for me and the rest was history.

A knock at the door pulled me from my thoughts and when I answered it, I had an unexpected visitor. "Marcus, oh my god, please tell me that Khalif came over here," Keisha stated in a frightened tone. I opened the door further so that she could walk inside and replied, "Nah Keish, lil nigga ain't been here. What the hell is going on?"

"Marcus, you gotta talk to him. He's been practicing his aim with that damn gun you gave him and talking about preparing himself. Dammit Marcus, I don't want him to grow up and be like his damn daddy. I don't want him to be a product of the fucking streets," She stated and shook her head. I could see the disappointment in her eyes and tried to calm her down. I put an arm around her and led her to the couch so she could sit down and said, "Keisha, I know what I'm about to tell you ain't what you wanna hear but that lil nigga is broken. His heart ain't gonna heal no time soon. It may not ever heal at all. The only thing that makes him feel better is thinking about revenge but that shit is all talk. He gonna be aight."

She looked at me crazy and said, "no the fuck he ain't gonna be alright. He ain't just thinking about revenge, he's gonna get it. He wants to kill that bitch you were fucking with; I can see it in his eyes. I mean, I ain't gonna lie, I'd love to beat that bitches ass but I'm not gonna sit back and lose my son to the streets. You're the only father figure he's had in his life Marcus, and I need you to step up and talk to him. Stop him from making a big mistake. I just still can't believe that you gave him that damn gun. Damn you, Marcus."

I leaned back and pulled Keisha to me and said, "Fuck that you talkin'. Shit, you know that lil mutha fucka gonna do what he wants to do no matter who talks to him. That's Feelow's son and his head is just as hard as his daddy's."

"That's fucked up for you to think that way Marcus, and when I find his bad ass, I'm taking that gun you gave him and hitting him upside the head with it. Maybe it will knock some sense into him.

"Oh yeah, I got a head you can knock some sense into. Come on and let a nigga get some of that slow neck," I said and unzipped my jeans. Keisha laughed at my comment but put her hand down in my boxers and pulled the python out. She got down on her knees in front of me and while she looked up into my eyes, she stuck her tongue out and licked the pre cum off of the tip.

"Yeah, Keisha. Put that muthafucka in your mouth just like old times. Make a nigga shoot something warm down ya throat," I said in pleasure when the head of my dick disappeared between her lips. I had never met a bitch that could suck a dick like Keisha. I reminisced back on the times we used to share. The times before she gave me an ultimatum, "for the right price, this pussy can be yours forever." It had been years but I would never forget how she worked her pussy on my rod.

I looked down at her and said "Take them pants off for me. A nigga know that shit good and wet."

She let my dick fall out of her mouth and instantly dropped her pants and thong. Her ass was still thick and her pussy lips were still fat. She spread her legs and straddled my lap and before she slid down on my pole, she said, "Nigga, I knew you missed this pussy. You know ain't no other bitch gonna ride this dick like me, not even the bitch you lay beside every night."

Keisha had her arms wrapped around my neck while I had mine on her hips. Her nipples were braless and looked like small bullets ready to split a niggas wig. I reached up and pinched one to bring her a little extra pleasure. "Yeah Keisha, ride that mutha fucka. Shit, that feels good." I said out loud while droplets of sweat formed on my face. I reached behind her and put a hand on each ass cheek and pushed up so I could meet her thrust for thrust.

Keisha began to talk shit and it made me feel like a beast, "All this good ass dick. Nigga fuck me like you mad. Shit, I don't ever wanna get off this mutha fucka. Yes Marcus, nigga, I needed this."

I leaned my head back and closed my eyes and enjoyed the feeling. Our bare skin clapped on each impact and I could feel my nuts swell as they prepared to shoot out the seeds they were full of. "I'm about to cum all in this pussy Keisha," I cried out and then, I felt her speed up, she tightened her pussy muscles around my thickness and caused my head to spin. I felt like I was on an amusement park ride and was about to go down the slope. Keisha had taken me to another world and I couldn't have escaped even if I'd wanted to. My nuts were ready to burst, "Yeah Keisha, shit. I'm about to …" but before I could finish my sentence I heard the front door slam.

"Marcus, what the fuck is going on in here?"

***

His black ass had some motherfuckin nerve to be fucking another bitch in our house, and of all bitches, it just had to be Keisha, my nemesis. "You fuckin bastard, how dare you, you're a piece of shit Marcus," I hollered out at him and the hoe on his dick. He pushed Keisha up off of him and I could see his dick shrivel up instantly. I couldn't believe his ass had the nerve to fuck her raw. Keisha acted like shit was okay but I ran up on that bitch and swung, "whoa, whoa, whoa Killi," Marcus said and grabbed my arm before I made contact.

"Get your fucking hands off of me Marcus so I can beat this bitch's ass," I cried out while tears formed in my eyes and threatened to blind me. I didn't want to cry in front of her but my heart was broken.

"Come on baby, please. Shit, I'm sorry, dammit, I don't even know how it happened," Marcus had the nerve to say and then he turned to Keisha and said, "get the fuck outta here Keisha."

She looked from me to Marcus and then said, "Okay, I'll leave but give me a call later on. I need to go find my son." Keisha bumped my shoulder when she walked past me and then slammed the door behind her. I turned to Marcus and gave him an angry look and asked, "Where the hell is Markill? What if he would have walked in on that foul shit? You ain't shit Marcus." I started to walk away so I could locate my son but Marcus grabbed my arm and pulled me back.

"That lil nigga is outside and I won't worry about him walking in. Shit, his ass is gonna be deep in a bitch one day too. Come on ma, a nigga apologizes. I don't even know how that shit happened." He stated with a smile but I was not impressed.

"I know how it happened. That dumb ass hoe done came over here with a sob story and did what she could to make you feel bad and then she took advantage of you. And what the hell did she mean about going to find her son? Is Khalif okay?" I had been through the motions of Marcus passing out dick like plates at a soup kitchen and had always forgiven him. My love for him was deep and I knew that one day, that love would be the death of me.

"Nah ma, Keisha caught Khalif playing with that pellet gun I gave him for his birthday and he told her that he was preparing himself."

"Preparing himself for what, Marcus?" I asked him. Keisha may have been my worst nightmare but I genuinely cared about Khalif. He was a good kid that came from bad stock. It wasn't his fault that he grew from a wilted flower. He couldn't help who his mother was. All the times he had come over and played with Markill, I could see potential in him; however, his blood line would never allow him to reach that potential fully.

"He told her that he was preparing himself to kill Krystal because she took his dad from him," Marcus said with his head held down. I know that he had thought a lot about the white girl that went to prison for him. However, I wasn't really sure of the type of thoughts he had of her. He claimed that she had meant nothing to him and at times I believed him but I could see it in his eyes.

I suddenly remembered why I had turned around and hurried home in the first place. "Oh my God, Marcus, I just remembered why I came back."

He looked at me funny and asked, "Oh yeah Killi, why did you turn back around?"

I answered him, "Her time is up Marcus, Krystal is getting out."

***

I looked at Killisha in shock before I sat down on the couch to absorb what she had told me. I palmed my caesar cut with both hands and asked, "Has it really been that long? Where the fuck did the time go?"

"Yes Marcus, it's been that long. You were on trial for Feelows murder and I was still pregnant with Markill when she confessed. Markill is about to be eleven," she said and then sat down beside me. Her care and concern for my well-being had always outweighed her own feelings. She had just walked in on me fucking another bitch and yet, she was worried about me. I leaned back on the couch and pulled her into my arms and said, "Baby, you don't have to worry about shit, not even Krystal. That bitch ain't dumb enough to come back here after confessing to killing a hood legend. Plus, she knows that no one wants her here, so she'll have nobody. The bitch is on her own. I can't think of anything that would make her want to come back here, so let's just keep living our lives, okay."

She snuggled in closer to me and said, "yeah, I guess you're right. I don't know why I'm so worried about her. I guess that I was a little afraid that she would show up and you'd fall right back in sync with her. You had to have had some type of feelings for her Marcus."

I sat up quickly and turned to her. I put a finger under her chin and pushed her head up enough for us to be eye to eye and said, "A nigga loves you Killi and I ain't going nowhere. You have been with me even before aloof this and I know that shit you caught me doing with Keisha is probably fucking with your mind but a nigga ain't leaving you. I know I do some foul shit sometimes but I always come home to you at night. Always. Do you understand?"

"Yeah Marcus, I do understand but I have an aching feeling that one night, you may not make it home at all, or even for that matter, you may not make it home ever again." I brushed a thumb under her eye to stop the tear that had fallen. Killisha had always been so strong and she had never been insecure. For some reason, she thought Krystal was going to be a threat. "Nothing can stop me from coming home to you. Nothing." I said. I only hoped that I was telling her the truth.

***

"Yo kill, my momma ain't over here, is she?" I asked in a whisper. I had cut through the woods to get to my uncle Marcus' house but I also knew that would be the first place my momma would look for me at. My mind had been made up and I didn't feel like hearing one of her lectures.

"Nah cuz. I think I heard her and my momma cursing each other out a little while ago but it's been quiet for a minute, so I think auntie Keisha left. Why are you dodging your moms like that? What's up with you?"

"Man, my momma trippin' bout that gun your dad gave me for my birthday but I ain't studying her ass. I'm trying to get my aim on point because I'm on a killing mission," I stated with enthusiasm.

"A killing mission. Man, who the hell are you trying to kill?" he asked me with a raised brow.

I told him the truth, "I plan on getting revenge for my daddy. My momma wants me to let that shit go but that ain't about to happen."

Markill shrugged and said, "Yeah, I feel you on that cuz but don't you think you should wait till you get older?" at least build yourself an army first."

"An army? Man, I 'ont need no damn army behind me. I'm an army all by myself and I can handle it solo. This shit is personal anyway," I stated angrily.

Markill shook his head and asked me, "Cuz, how do you know that chic gonna even come back this way?"

I gave him a crazy look and said, "Man, I know when she gets out, she's gonna eventually pop back up. That white bitch left something behind and I feel like she's gonna come back to get it."

"Cuz, you trippin. What could she have possibly left behind?"

I answered his question with a look of death in my eyes, "Your daddy nigga. She left your daddy behind."

Chapter Two

The ride from the prison to the bus station seemed to take hours when really it was only twenty minutes away. When the van pulled in, I looked around at all the people and wondered what stories they had to tell. Were they dropped off there by a prison guard or was it something else?" Alright Madison, you're a free woman now. Good luck out there," The transport officer said with a smile but she was the only one happy.

"Yeah, thanks," I stated and got out of the van. I walked to the counter to get my ticket punched and was then told where to go to board my bus.

I stepped onto the bus nervous as hell and found a seat by the window. After everyone else had boarded, I was thankful that no one sat in the seat beside me because I just needed to be alone. I didn't need some stranger trying to be friendly and asking questions. It began to rain outside, and I leaned my head against the window and watched it fall. When I was growing up, my father had always told me, "when it rains, it means that the angels in heaven are crying." I wondered who had upset them to make them cry so many tears. The sounds of the rain pelting against the bus seemed to put me at ease and made me fall into a deep sleep.

I could feel his touch and it felt so good. "Oh baby, I missed you so much." He said to me and then took his time kissing down bare skin. When he got to my most sacred place, he spread my legs and took me to a world that had been foreign to me for a while. "Yes, oh yes baby. Please don't stop." I had never felt anything so good in my life. I gripped the back of his head and pushed it into my garden. I wanted to suffocate him with my love because he was the only one who deserved it. I could feel myself about to cum but before I had the chance to explode, I was brought back to reality.

"Excuse me miss, but this is as far as the bus goes. You're going to have to get off," I heard the voice but my mind couldn't register what was being said. I opened my eyes and then turned my head to look at him but ignored him and turned my head back to the window.

"Miss, you have to get off the bus. I'm sorry," he stated one more time. I turned my head and faced him again but saw a face that I could never forget.

"Marcus. You bastard. How could you do that to me?" How could you just leave me for dead like that after all I done for you?" I could feel the tears form and wondered if the angels cried from a broken heart like mine.

"Miss, are you alright? Is there someone you need me to call for you?"

I heard the driver's voice again and snapped out of it. I wiped the tears away when I realized that it was not Marcus in front of me. "Oh my god, I am sorry," I stated and grabbed my small bag. I jumped up from the seat and accidentally bumped into the driver as I rushed past him. I ran down the two small steps that would put me out the door and stopped. The rain pelted against my skin but I couldn't will myself to move. I enjoyed the wetness from the sky as the angels poured down their headache onto me. I looked around at all the people but could only see one face; "Dammit Krys, get it together."

I found the women's restroom and walked inside so that I could get away from the crowd. I found an empty stall and sat down on the toilet so that I could get my emotions in check. I heard a tap on the stall door and opened it to a pregnant woman standing there, "Are you okay? I heard you in here and wondered if there was something I could do for you." She asked.

"No um. Thanks, but I'm just enjoying my newfound free-dom." She looked at me puzzled so I made up a quick line like," I just got out of a very bad relationship and I'm just so happy that I can finally move on with my life."

"Well, alright then. As long as you're okay," she said and turned to leave. I looked at the small bump in front of her and my heart broke. I thought about the baby that Marcus had made me get rid of and the stomach of the other woman that he had lovingly caressed the day I was taken from the courthouse. I wondered where that woman and child were at today and hoped that they didn't get in the way when I went for Marcus because if they did, I would not spare them. That bastard owed me and I was going to get paid one way or the other.

***

"Do you ever think about her?"

"What?"

"Krystal, do you ever think about her?"

Carrie's question caught me off guard because it wasn't one that I had expected, "Can't you just help me package this shit up without opening your fucking mouth? Ain't Jambo taught you anything?"

Carrie had become a crucial part of my operation over the years and the fact that she was my right-hand woman saved her from a lot of cursing out. She was a good person but sometimes, her ass talked too damn much, "come on B, you can tell me. I'm not going to run back and tell Mya that you've been thinking about the next bitch, so don't worry about that. I'm just curious."

"Do I look like I give a fuck about you telling Mya shit, she ain't my damn momma, the fuck?"

"No, she ain't your momma but right now she is the bitch that's claiming you."

I looked at Carrie sideways and said "nah, I don't ever think about her ass. She made her decision when she took that shit for that nigga. Fuck, I look like thinking about a bitch like that?" Now let's finish this shit so we can get it delivered and I can step my ass out for good."

The truth was, I had never stopped thinking about Krystal. She had been gone many years and never once reached out to me. I had given her my number when we first met and promised her that it would never change and I kept my word. I met Mya a couple of years after Krystal was gone and although she couldn't compare, she was a doable substitute, but as hard as I tried, I couldn't give her my heart or forever because all that belonged to someone else.

Corey Robinson

"Ya know my daddy would roll over in his grave if he knew that I was standing her packaging up kilos of cocaine."

"Carrie's father had been a police detective who had been shot down in a drug bust. He had never agreed with her choices but Carrie did her own thing regardless of what anyone said. Her dad was the main reason I couldn't trust her but over the years, she proved her loyalty.

"Maybe you should think about changing professions."

"Nah, I'm too damn good at it. I actually think that this is what I was born to do."

I shook my head and said, "bitch, you truly are crazy." I taped up the last brick that I would ever lay my hands on. I was retiring from the game I had been in almost all of my life. I was going to pass the reins to my right-hand Jambo and then sit back and enjoy the fruits of my labor. I only wished that I had someone to share it with.

The door suddenly opened and Jambo walked in with a surprise, "come on Jam, we family man. I swear I'm gonna pay you back the money. Please just give me a chance." Karmel cried out but Jambo didn't have compassion, not even for family when it came to our money.

"Bitch nigga, you shoulda never fucked off with my bread, who the hell do you think you are? I've slit niggas throats for less than what you owe me, so how the hell you figure I'm supposed to let you ride?" Jambo shouted while he held his nine-millimeter to Karmel's head.

"Jam, a nigga just got caught up but I swear, if you'll give me a chance, I'll have you paid off in a few days. I'll get you your money man. Please. Come on, I got kids cuz," Karmel continued to plead for his life as sweat and tears ran down his face.

"You weren't thinking 'bout them little crumb snatchers when you tricked off my fuckin money. Shit, them little bastards are probably better off without you. I pay you good nigga and yet, your ass still wants more." Jambo said and then dragged Karmel out of the room. He shut the door behind them but I and Carrie

22

could still hear Karmel's cries. I had never seen Jambo spare a nigga about our money, so I wondered what decision he was going to make about his cousin. Karmel had fucked around and started gambling and it had gotten the best of him. His money had been coming up short for a while. Jambo kept brushing it off but when I heard the shot, I knew that wasn't letting it go anymore. Karmel would now be dog food to Carrie's two mastiffs, Hey-Man and Karma. The two dogs were older now but they still had the same vicious appetite.

"Ya know, I still think about him," Carrie said once the room grew quiet.

"I'm talking about Creston. I really did love him but he just wouldn't love me back. He needed other women no matter how much I satisfied him. But I'm happy now. Jambo makes me very happy. My ass is still crazy although it's now a different kind of crazy."

I had never met Creep, the nigga she was talking about but it felt like I had because when she first showed up at the door, that was all she rapped about. She didn't shut up until Jambo laid the pipe on her. I had told Jambo that if he wanted to keep her, then he'd have to do it somewhere else. There wasn't no way I was taking the chance of police busting in my door. I didn't know how close Carrie and her daddy dearest were and I wasn't taking any chances, but as the years passed and her loyalty to my boy showed, my guard slowly dropped.

Jambo suddenly appeared back in the room and said, "well, at least the kids have been fed," referring to the dogs.

"Nigga, you ain't shit, your own damn cousin?" I said and shook my head. I had always let him handle the dirty work because that was why I'd hired him in the first place. However, on occasion, I got my hands dirty too but not as often as my boy. "Aight let's load up the ride so I can get outta this mutha fucka. I'm almost to freedom," I said with a smile and held my hands up in the air as if I were surrendering.

We all walked out the back door to get to the garage where the jet-black Lincoln Navigator was waiting. Jambo removed the front grill and we packed it with one hundred kilos of the best Colombian cocaine. Carrie would drive the Navigator to the mall and park it right next to an identical one that would be packed with the money. She would leave the keys in the pocket of the driver's side door and go inside where she would grab a quick bite to eat from one of the delis. I and Jambo would be parked across the street and keep watch to make sure nothing went wrong. Carrie would come out of the mall, jump in the other vehicle and drive to the money house. We'd all get our cut and then go our separate ways.

We had been doing it that way for years and never had an issue at any location we chose to make the witch at. At first, we were against Carrie putting herself out there like that but she assured us she could handle it and we knew that she could be trusted. I was glad that Jambo found a bitch he could vibe with because he had been by himself for so long.

When I pulled up in my driveway, I saw Mya's car parked in it. I had never given her a key to my crib because I didn't consider her wifey material. I wasn't gonna have no bitch making extra copies of my key, so if I broke it off, they would still have access to my life. That shit wasn't about to happen. I also didn't like the fact of her just showing up at my door and not calling ahead of time. I watched as she got out of her car and swayed my way. Her Ivy Park jeans formed to her shape like they had been painted on, and the matching Ivy Park t-shirt she had tied up in a knot on the side gave me a peek at her toned stomach. Her long hair was loose and gave her an exotic look. I ain't gonna lie, the bitch was bad but she just wasn't the one my heart truly wanted.

"Hey baby. I have been waiting for you," she said as soon as I opened my car door.

"Sup?" I asked and got out.

"Mmm, okay, I sense that you really don't want to be bothered but I'm a hard-headed bitch."

"Yeah Mya, you are hard-headed," I stated as I walked past her, "Didn't I tell your ass to call before you showed up over here?" I walked into the condo I had purchased a few years after Krystal went to prison. I needed a change of scenery because everything at my house reminded me of her. None of the bitches I fucked over the years had ever been to my house, only the condo, Mya followed behind me closely and said, "you should sit down and relax baby. Let Mya make you feel better."

I sat down on the couch and kicked my Timberlands off my feet and watched as Mya walked over to me seductively. She stopped in front of me and pulled her shirt and bra off exposing her perfect breast. Her dark brown nipples were hard and ready and I felt my dick jump when she put her fingers around them and twisted. She smiled at me but I wasn't flattered. I cared a lot about her just not enough to give a fuck at that moment. She pulled down her shorts and thong before she dropped to her knees in front of me and unzipped my jeans. When she went to reach into my boxers, I pushed her hand away and said, "Nah Mya, a nigga really ain't in the mood right now. I just wanna chill."

I knew that my reason for not being in the mood had to do with the talk I'd had with Carrie. Ever since she mentioned Krystal, I couldn't get her out of my mind. Mya could never fully satisfy me no matter how hard she tried or how many times we fucked. I had only been with Krystal once and I ain't found a bitch yet that could fill her spot.

"Come on Brandon, I'm so horny right now baby, at least let me taste you."

She reached for my boxers again but this time, I didn't stop her. I'd let her annoying ass find out for herself. I closed my eyes when she pulled the head of my dick between her lips but it wasn't from pleasure. I closed them so I could imagine Krystal in front of me. I could see her face so clearly and it made me smile. If only she would have listened to me and done what I told her, she could have been the one on my dick right then instead of Mya's ass.

Marcus only wanted her so she could be used as his dope mule. He had never given a fuck about her. When I found out that he had allowed her to take the rap for his shit, I made up an excuse and cut his punk ass off. There was no way that I could have still dealt with him without thoughts of killing him. I had told myself many times over the years to reach out to Krystal but I didn't because she had made her choice to ride with Marcus instead of me. She knew how to find me if she wanted to and if she ever did, I'd welcome her with open arms.

My dick was hard as a steel pole and I could feel my nut sack tighter with anticipation. "Yeah Krystal. Baby do that shit." I cried out in pleasure with my eyes still closed.

"Nigga who the fuck is Krystal?" Mya asked with an attitude when she let my dick fall out of her mouth. I opened my eyes and looked at her and my dick shriveled up instantly.

"Yo, come on ma, just finish, you hearing shit," I said but I could tell by the look in her eyes that I wouldn't be getting that nut.

"You know what Brandon? I'm done with your no-good ass. I'm trying to make you feel good after a long day and you got the nerve to call me by another bitch's name. I'm tired of trying to please you. I've been trying for years to be everything you need but your fuck ass doesn't deserve a bitch like me. So whoever the fuck this Krystal bitch is, let that hoe suck that mutha fucka because my ass is outta here fuck boy," Mya exclaimed and then put her clothes back on and rushed out leaving me with my dick still hanging out.

"Man, fuck you," I said out loud after Mya slammed the door behind herself.

I put my dick back in my boxers and got up so that I could go take a shower and crash for the night. I went into my dresser drawer and pulled out a sac of kush and a blunt so I could roll one up before I rinsed off. I sparked up the spliff and took a long hand pull and then another thought came to my mind. "Oh shit," I said out loud and put out the kush I was smoking. The time had finally come and I needed to make sure that I was ready, just in case.

***

I was chilling outside of the trap house when Tammy's crack-head ass walked up and disturbed my peace. She looked like she hadn't bathed in days and the truth was, she probably hadn't.
"Sup Tammy? I hope you ain't here on no bullshit."

She licked her dry cracked lips and pulled a few crumpled-up dollar bills out of her bra and said, "look Rap, I only got about five dollars right now but I need a wake-up to get me going, can you help me out?"

"Nah, bitch, what you need is a fuckin' shower. When is the last time your ass bathed?"

Tammy had always been ghetto but the bitch had done good for herself. She had always managed to hold down good-paying jobs with top positions. Niggas everywhere sweated her ass but now, she didn't even have an ass to sweat. The crack had taken everything from her. Tammy was Keisha's cousin and I knew that at one time, they had fallen out because Tammy wanted Feelow for herself. She had even fucked him behind Keisha's back. However, the death of Feelow had changed a lot of shit, including Tammy. She picked up the pipe to hide her pain and was never able to put it down. Now she was a product of the streets and didn't have shit.

"Well, if you'll just give me a wake-up, I'll go and take a shower as soon as I do it. Come on Trap, I need something to get me going."

I knew that she was lying because it's the same with all crack-heads. One hit only leads to another hit; she would never make it to a shower, so I gave her an ultimatum.

"I'll tell you what I will do for you. I'll give you a whole fifty pack if you go take a shower and put on some fresh clothes. If you don't wanna do that, then you can go suck a dick and get that wake-up."

Her eyes grew big in anticipation of receiving a whole fifty pack. She stated, 'alright Trap, I'm a do what you asked but don't play no games and fuck me over. I'm a hold you to your word."

"Now Tammy, when have you known me to not be a man of my word?" Do as I asked and I promise, I got you. No, go head on, I'm a sit right here and wait on you."

"Alright, I'll be back in a couple of minutes."

"Oh hell no, you betta wash that ass longer than a couple of minutes. Don't make me get my boy to do a finger check on that pussy to make sure it's fresh." I hollered out when Tammy ran off to do what I'd asked of her. About that time, Creep walked out the door and sat in the chair beside mine and said, "nigga, I heard you're no good ass and my fingers ain't going no where near that rank ass pussy. Bitch, you got me fucked up, I ain't tryin' to have to get my shits amputated from sticking them up in that. That pussy is probably full of gangrene." The two of us shared a laugh at his comment.

"Aye man, I unjust got off the phone with Marcus. That dumb ass nigga got caught with Keisha on his dick." Creep stated.

"What? Hell no, that mutha fucka let Killi walk in on him with Keisha? Man, that's some foul-ass shit. I ain't even know he was fuckin' with Keisha like that again. His ass ratchet as hell."

"Yeah dawg, that's a dumb ass mutha fucka. If I had a bitch like Killi on my arm, I wouldn't neva stick my dick in nothing else," Creep stated with a smile on his face! It was no secret that he had a secret crush on Killisha but he would never act on it out of respect for Marcus.

I was shocked that Marcus would fuck with Keisha like that again after all he had been through with Feelow. It didn't matter that Fee was gone, Keisha is his baby momma and that alone made her off-limits. However, Marcus didn't give a fuck about respecting boundaries. His ass had always felt like the world belonged to him. Everyone else was just taking up space in it.

I knew that Killisha would forgive him even though she hated Keisha. He had been caught with his pants down many times and she always forgave him like him fucking other bitches was okay, so he continued to do so.

Not even ten minutes had passed and I saw Tammy as she walked back up the road to pick up her fifty packs. I was gonna take that bitch inside the house and do a panty check on her to make sure her shit was fresh. If I smelled anything foul, that bitch wasn't gonna get shit from me.

I stood so I could meet her at the steps but before she made it all the way to the yard, Keisha pulled up and I knew that there was about to be some drama, and it would be more than any of us were ready for.

"Where the fuck is that bitch going? I know her crackhead ass ain't about to come see yall," Keisha questioned as soon as she got out of her car. She slammed the car door and placed both of her hands on her hips so she could keep an eye on Tammy, but the look on Keisha's face wasn't enough to stop Tammy's mission.

Tammy walked right past her cousin and came straight to me," Okay Trap, this pussy is good and fresh now. You wanna give it a test run?"

"Nah, I think I'll pass on that," I stated and looked her up and down. Tammy cleaned up very well and you could still see the taxes of her former self. I pulled the fifty packs out of my pocket and handed it to her as promised. "Here you go Tammy, make sure you smoke that shit slow so you don't bust your heart. Okay."

"Okay, thanks Trap, I'm outta here."

As soon as she turned around to walk away, Keisha stepped in front of her. "Bitch, why is your ass even over here?"

"Fuck you Keisha, I don't answer to your ass. Besides, neither of them niggas belong to you, so you don't run shit over here."

"Yeah, well they don't belong to you either. They don't want your begging, disloyal ass over here, so go the fuck on and find somewhere else to cop your shit at."

Keisha pushed past Tammy but before she could reach the top step, Tammy went in on her, "disloyal? Bitch, you are the one still on Marcus' nut sack. Walking around acting like you still grieving over the loss of Feelow but yet, you are letting his best friend slide in his zone."

"Bitch, you don't know shit about me or what the hell I do," Keisha replied and pushed Tammy lightly.

"Aye yo. Yo yall bitches gotta chill or take that shit somewhere else. Yall gonna bring the muthafucking heat with that shit," I said to them but Creep was on a different level.

"Nah nigga, let them hoes scrap. Shit, I ain't seen a good catfight in a long time. Hell, I'm putting my money on Tammy's ass. One hit of that shit and she's gon' go ape on Keisha's ass."

I gave Creep a foul look and said, "Chill dawg, you wanna see these bitches fight, you gonna have to go somewhere else. That shit ain't gonna happen here." I turned back to the women and put a hand on each of their shoulders so I could put some space between them, but although it would stop any physical contact, the words still spewed from their mouths.

Keisha exclaimed, "bitch, you're just mad cause Feelow chose me over you."

"Huh, chose you. Yeah whatever, I guess that explains why his nutsack was tapping this ass while he was deep in this pussy; bitch, you were just convenient. He was only using you to get closer to Marcus so he could take him out, and you were game. Now you wanna act like he means so much to your snake ass." I looked at Tammy and absorbed the words that had left her mouth and then turned to Keisha. 'Trap, don't listen to her. I would never do no shit like that and go against Marcus, not for nobody."

"Yeah, well Trap, you can believe what you want to believe but this bitch is a snake and she'll turn on yall too. Her ass was in cahoots with Feelow and she had planned on seducing Marcus so Fee could catch him with his pants down," Tammy stated with raised eyebrows.

Keisha said convincingly, "bitch, they'll never take your word over mine. Trap and Creep both know that I'm down for Marcus and I would never do anything to hurt him. He and I are closer than ever."

"So you still gonna be loyal to the enemy? I bet Feelow rolling over in his grave right now looking down at your disrespectful ass."

"Yo Keisha, is that shit true?" were you gonna set my nigga up so Feelow could take him out?" I asked.

Creep wanted the answer too, "yeah Keisha, did you try to snake Marcus? Please tell me that Tammy's ass is lying."

Keisha looked at all three of us but didn't answer the question. Her silence answered it for us though, "you know what? I don't have time for this shit. I only came over here to look for my son. So if yall haven't seen him, I'll be on my way." Keisha exclaimed and walked to her car. She opened her car door to get in but before she had a chance to get inside, Tammy said something that would change her world forever.

Corey Robinson

Chapter Three

I took a look out the back window and watched as Markill and Khalif talked. I thought about what Keisha had told me and decided that maybe I should talk to both boys. I was grooming my son to take over the streets when I retired but Khalif didn't have to be groomed because he was born with it in his blood. I was about to slide the glass doors open when I heard someone at my front door.

"I got it Marcus," Killisha yelled out but I decided to go and see who it was along with her. Neither one of us was expecting company and in my line of work, sometimes the unexpected is not a good thing.

"Where in the hell is Marcus?" Keisha asked as soon as Killisha had the door open.

"Bitch, my man doesn't answer to you, who in the hell do you think you are coming to my front door and asking for him like you running something?"

"I'm not here to argue with your dumb ass Killisha. I need to see Marcus."

Before Killisha could respond, I pushed her to the side and looked Keisha in the face. "What the fuck is wrong with you na? Why the hell are you showing up at my shit and showing out?" I asked angrily. If I would have known that sticking my dick to her would make her act like that, I never would have gotten it wet.

Keisha put her hands on her hips and asked, "is it true Marcus?" She was on the verge of tears but I had no idea what the hell she was talking about.

"What the fuck are you talking about? Is what true?"

She looked from me to Killisha like she was nervous. I told my girl to let me handle it and she gave me a crazy look but walked away. When Killisha was out of sight, Keisha asked, "did you have something to do with Feelow getting killed? Please Marcus, I deserve the truth."

I watched the tears fall from her saddened eyes but those tears didn't mean shit to me. I had kept my involvement with Feelows murder on the low for over ten years and I planned to keep it that way. Only a couple of my most trusted soldiers knew about it, so I wondered where she had gotten her information from.

"Keisha, your ass is trippin', who the hell told you some shit like that?"

"Just answer the fucking question Marcus. Did you have something to do with my son's father getting killed?"

"Nah Keisha, I ain't had shit to do with that. Bitch, you should know me better than that. What the fuck do I look like killing him?"

"You and Feelow had some beef going on that yall never really severed. You had caused Marcus, you knew that he had come for you and was coming again. I need to know if you struck back."

"Didn't I just tell your ass that I ain't had shit to do with that? You think I'm so heartless that I could kill him when he was like a brother to me? No matter how much beef we had, I could never bring him any harm or allow anyone else to bring it."

"You let that white bitch get close and look what happened, I'm not dumb Marcus. I know the code of the streets. Disloyalty brings death among crews, even those that are like family."

"Keisha, you trippin for real."

"Am I really, Marcus?"

I had been standing in the doorway but finally stepped out and shut the door behind me. Keisha sat down on the front steps so I sat down beside her. I needed to drill her so I could find out who made her feel the way she did. There was no statute of limitations on murder and if someone was talking after so many years had passed, I needed to know who it was, so I could take care of the problem.

"I and my cousin Tammy had got into it. I ran into her over at Trap and Creeps and we passed some words. Before I left, she hollered out that she watched you beat Feelow and then shoot him in the head. She told me that I was sleeping with the enemy, and I needed to make sure that I wasn't."

"Tammy huh? And you believed her and then had the nerve to come over here and question me about that shit. Come on Keisha.

What the fuck is going on with you? Shit, Fee is up there resting peacefully, so rest your nerves and don't dwell on bullshit."

"Yeah Marcus, you're right, I'm sorry I even came over here and asked you something like that. I should have known better. Tammy knew that hearing something like that would hurt me and dammit, it worked. I hope you're not too mad at me."

I pulled Keisha into me for a hug to let her know that everything was good and then said, "Aye, go ahead and get outta here before I gotta pull Killi off your ass again."

We shared a laugh and she replied, "I'm going to apologize ahead of time for disrespecting you but one day, I'm a beat that bitches ass."

I knew that Keisha meant what she said and wished that there was something I could do to make them get along. However, as long as Keisha was sweatin' my dick game, they would never be cordial. I walked Keisha to her car and remembered that Khalif was in my backyard playing with Markill.

"Oh yeah, ya boy in the back with Kill. He showed up a little after you left. I'm a have that talk with him and then I'll bring him to you. Maybe we can finish what we started earlier."

"Yeah before your bitch busted in," she said flirtatiously.

"Yeah right. Go get that thang ready for me. I'm a make you forget everything your mind is on."

Keisha smiled and then started her car.

As soon as she pulled off, I pulled my cell out of my pocket and called Toe Tag. I needed to take care of my little problem before it festered and took care of me instead.

***

Every word out of his mouth was a lie. I could tell, but my momma didn't know any better. She was too mesmerized by my uncle Marcus' charm but I could see straight through his ass.

I had heard my momma's voice while she argued with my auntie Killi. They had never gotten along but although they hated each other, they both loved me. I walked around the corner of the house when I heard them but stayed in the cut so they wouldn't see me. I was shocked when momma asked him about my daddy's murder and I could tell that he was too. While she waited for an answer, I already had mine. I could read people very well and it was hard to get anything past me.

I trusted my uncle Marcus and looked up to him; he had been the only father figure I'd ever had and he taught me a lot from a young age. I had just turned eleven but had enough street sense to outsmart the best of them. It broke my heart to think that I had to question his loyalty, not only to me but to my daddy. If I found out that he was the reason I grew up without my pops, it would be bad for him.

When I saw my uncle Marcus go back in the house, I ran back around to where Markill was. He had my pellet gun in his hands and I snatched it with force from him.

"Man, what the hell is wrong with you?" Kill asked me with a confused look.

"You ain't ready for one of these cuz. You gotta get your gangsta up before you can hold this," I said and pointed the gun at a can. I pulled the trigger and hit the can dead on.

"Nigga, my gangsta is already up. My daddy is the king of the streets. I was born into the life."

I could do nothing but laugh because Markill was a soft-ass nigga. He would have to toughen up before he could go on a caper with me. We both turned around when we heard the back door slide open. Uncle Marcus walked out with a box in his hand and stood in front of Markill.

"I know your birthday is right around the corner but I wanted to go ahead and give you one of your gifts," he said and then handed the box to Kill.

Markill opened it up quickly and said excitedly, "ah, thanks dad. Now I and Khalif can practice target shooting together."

I was happy that Kill got his own gun because I didn't like seeing mine in his hand. I was still feeling some type of way about my uncle, so I didn't say anything. I guess he noticed my apprehension and asked, "Yo Khalif, yo good lil nigga?"

"Yeah. I'm straight."

He turned to Kill and told him, "Aye son, go in the house and show your momma what you got. Tell her that I'll be in soon. I just gotta holler at Khalif for a minute."

"Alright dad, but are you gonna teach me how to shoot this thing?" Kill asked him proudly.

"Damn right I am. I'm a take you and Khalif to the beginners range tomorrow. Teach yall lil niggas how to pop off," Uncle Marcus stated before Kill ran inside.

He turned back to me and asked, "So what's on ya mind 'Lif?"

I looked at him with murder in my eyes and said, "Remember when you taught me how to read a man and tell if he's lying?"

"Yeah, I remember, and you aced it."

"Uncle Marcus, I heard my momma talking to you earlier. I crept around the house and heard her ask you about my daddy. You see Uncle Marcus, my momma will believe almost anything you tell her but I'm not impressed."

"Lil nigga, why don't you just go ahead and spit out what you trying to say, 'cause I got a feeling that I ain't gonna like it."

"You lied to my momma today." I blurted out.

"What the hell are you talking about nigga, I don't gotta lie about shit and I don't gotta explain myself to an eleven-year-old kid."

I nodded my head and knew that I had busted him. I knew that I read him right but he still tried to convince me of different. "You lied but until I can prove it, I'm a let you slide."

"Oh, you call yourself threatening me? Do you know who the fuck I am and what I'm capable of lil nigga? Huh? You betta stay in a child's place. Now get your ass up so I can take you home to your momma. I'ma give you the rest of the night to get your mind right and then I'll talk to you. Who the fuck do you think you talking to?" Uncle Marcus exclaimed and then jumped up and pulled out his burner and said, "lil nigga, you betta not underestimate me because you got that toy gun in your possession. Betta grow your ass the fuck up before you threaten a grown ass man."

He then walked inside the house but a minute later, he poked his head back out and said, "come on so I can take your stupid ass home, and you better stay your ass there this time."

I let out a long sigh and got up so I could meet him in the car. I knew that I should have kept my thoughts to myself until I could prove something. I hoped that I was wrong about him because if I wasn't, our relationship would never be the same again. Uncle Marcus was the only father I'd ever had in my life but to avenge my daddy's death, I would feed him a bullet too. I knew that I was still too young to go to war with a grown man but as soon as I got my shit on point, I was going to ask him about my daddy's death once again and he better hope that I believe him.

***

"Aye man, who was that on the phone?" Echo asked me after I'd hung up.

"It was Marcus. He says he got a job for me." I stated.

My boy Echo and Marcus had been rivals for many years. Their beef was over a bitch that neither of them ended up being with. About eleven years ago, I'd wanted to kill Marcus myself because I was led to believe that he'd killed Carla, the only woman I'd ever felt anything for. When I found out the truth, I felt like shit.

We had all ended up squashing the beef between us and went into business together. Echo became the supplier, I became the Muscle and Swag T, the female of the crew became the runner since our dope came from Brooklyn. The main supplier was her people and because they fucked with her, we had an in.

"Who is that nigga trying to get at now?" Swag T asked when she walked into the room. Her girlfriend of the month walked in behind her and I looked at Swag like she had lost her mind. Swag noticed and said to the woman, "Aye yo' baby. Why don't you go down to the store and pick us up some blunts so we can blow one." She handed her a few bills and sent her on her way.

When she was gone, I told them what Marcus had revealed to me, "he wants me to take out Tammy Watson."

"Aye, ain't that Keisha's cousin. Bitch gonna trip if her cousin gets killed," Swag stated.

"Yeah, it's her cousin but them hoes fell out years ago because of Feelow. Tammy wanted him but Keisha had him. Two bitches shoulda just shared the dick if you ask me," Echo said with a smile. "Shit, Keisha probably wants to kill her herself."

Swag asked, "so, what did she do to Marcus? Why does he want to knock her off?"

"Keisha ran into her over at the bottom and they got into an argument. Tammy told Keisha that Marcus killed Feelow instead of the white girl. Keisha went and confronted him but he played that shit off. Now, that nigga is afraid that Tammy gonna tell more than Keisha and he doesn't want that shit open back up."

"How the hell did Tammy's cracked-out ass come up with some shit like that?" Sway asked with a confused look on her face.

I replied, "she was the eye witness but she had been too scared to take the stand against Marcus. Guess the bitch don grow some balls. Anyway, I'm a go get my shit together and then go in search of a crackhead."

I got up and went to get my weapon and extra ammo. I had planned to go to the block and proposition Tammy with some dope so she would ride with me. I was going to let her get her last good hit in and then make her ass suck my dick and as soon as I bust in her mouth I was gonna blow that hoe's brains out.

"Aight yall, I'ma be back after I handle this," I said and went to the front door to leave. Swag's friend walked in at the same time I was leaving and stopped in front of me. I tried to push past her but she reached out and grabbed my dick and said, "I do still like dick ya know."

I grabbed her hand and squeezed it hard enough to make her flinch and said, "nah, I'm good and when I get back, make sure your ass is gone because if you're still here, pussy will be the last thing you remember."

Corey Robinson

I rushed out the door after I threatened her and knew that it would be the last time I saw her. The only woman me and Swag fucked together was the ones that neither of us claimed. I knew that Swag had taken a liking to her so that meant she was off limits but I'd be damned if I'd let a disloyal bitch lie beside my sister. I'd let Swag know what went down when I got back. I jumped in my ride and headed to the bottom where I knew Tammy hung out at.

I knew from a young age that I'd been born to be a killer. It was something that I enjoyed. The dope game wasn't really my thing, I'd rather bust a cap instead. My dick got hard every time I went on a job and it didn't go down until my mission was complete. I had met Echo when he first started out in the dope game. I was a jack boy but Echo saw potential in me and asked me if I'd like to work for him instead of taking the chances I was taking. I played hard at first because I didn't really trust another mutha fucka with my life. However, Echo didn't give up and I also knew that he was legit. I knew that every time I ran up on a dope boy, my life was at stake even after I walked away, so I ended up taking Echo up on his offer.

I pulled up to the bottom and saw all the crack fiends hanging around the house they all went to smoke at. I didn't get out because I didn't want anyone to remember my face. I had traded out my car before I made it this way, so that way, no one could identify it either. After I handled my business, the car would be taken to the chop shop and stripped. The next time I got in that car, it would look totally different.

I had sat and watched the house that I knew Tammy frequented but never saw her. "Man, this is some bullshit. Where the hell is this hoe at?" I stated out loud. I was tired of sitting there waiting, so I started the car back up and decided to try again the next night. However, as soon as I put the car in gear, I saw Tammy walk out of the house.

She stood in the yard of the crack house for a minute and looked around as if she were waiting on someone. I was about to pull up closer to the yard and approach her but instead, she began to walk off.

I pulled out and followed closely behind her. When she got far enough away from the house I pulled up beside her and let down the window. Tammy didn't know who I was but she would soon find out.

"Sup lil mama, you lookin' to have some fun?" I asked her and pulled out the small bag of dope that I got off of Echo before I left.

Tammy looked at me curiously and then bent down to the window and said "I don't usually just hop into cars like that especially with a nigga I ain't neva seen before."

I had made it my business to not be in the streets a lot because I didn't want my face known just in case I had run up on a mutha fuck; I usually stayed in the background and that worked for me.

"Shit, I'm tryna' to be a nigga you see right now. I know your ass wanna have a good time."

She smiled and said flirtatiously, "how I know you can give me a good time. That dope is only gonna make my mind feel good, what you got to make this pussy feel right?"

I grabbed her hand and pulled it to my dick so she could feel the beast I was gonna unleash on her and asked, "Is this enough to make that pussy right?"

"Hmmm, I might be able to work with that," She said with a smile and then stood up so she could walk around and get in the car with me.

I had never personally known Tammy but had seen her a lot around the way. She was a pretty girl and although she was hooked on that shit, I could tell that she had potential. I don't know what it was about crackheads but I could see things in them that no one else could. Looking at Tammy reminded me of Carla and I almost lost focus. I drove away from the curb I picked her up on and decided to get a room instead of using the car.

"Whoa, this is a nice ass hotel to bring a trick to. Must be my lucky night." She said and was about to get out but I grabbed her wrist and stopped her.

I pulled out a wad of cash and gave it to her and said, "go in the office and get a room for the night, and you better bring our ass right back! Don't make me come look for you because you won't like what will happen when I find you."

"Trust me, I know a good thing when I see it and I would be a fool to fuck it up. I smoke crack but I'm not stupid by a long shot." She said and got out.

About ten minutes had passed and she came back with the room key and said, "Come on, we're on the second floor."

I got out and followed behind her and we went to the room. When she opened the door she seemed to be amazed by its beauty. I might have been a killer but I still liked nice things.

"Why don't you go take a shower? I'll set you up right when you get out."

"Okay. Um, you think I could get a small taste first?"

I stared her down and my gut told me that she was straight up, so I gave her the package. I sat down in a chair and watched as she filled up her pipe. I thought of Carla again and was pissed at myself for not being able to save her. I wouldn't make that mistake again. Something inside of me had changed from the moment I first spoke to the woman in front of me.

Before she took a hit she asked me, "why are you staring at me like that?"

I didn't respond to her question but instead, I stated, "enjoy yourself. We got all night."

Tammy put the pipe to her lips and struck the lighter but before she put the flame to its end, she locked eyes with me. I had picked her up to take her breath away but instead, she had taken mine and I knew that I wouldn't be able to pull through.

Chapter Four

I knew that I probably should have tried the number before I just showed up but I was already there and refused to turn around. My heart sped up with each step I took. I didn't know if I was still welcome or not and honestly, I didn't give a damn.

I walked to the front window and tried to peek inside but the privacy screens were in place and allowed me to see nothing. It made me wonder if he was alone and my heart broke at the thought of someone else in his arms. I knew that I didn't deserve to be there but I couldn't will myself to leave.

I approached the front door and located the fake brick. I lifted it and saw that the extra key was still where he told me it would be. I couldn't believe that after all the years that had passed, everything was just as he told me it would always be.

My hand shook as I pushed the key into the lock and turned slowly. The door opened with ease and I walked in and shut it behind me. I stood against the door frame and inhaled lightly. His aroma filled the air and brought my body such pleasure. I couldn't believe that he still had that effect on me. I made my way to the staircase and took off my shoes before I walked up. My feet sunk into the plush carpet and made me feel as if I were walking among the clouds. When I got to the top of the steps, my next destination was the bedroom he had brought me such pleasure in. When I opened the door, I could hear the shower water running in the bathroom. I smiled at the thought of touching his nakedness. His body was so perfect. Every muscle formed just right.

I walked over to the king-size bed we had made love in and asked myself how I could leave all of that behind. I picked up the pillow he lay his head on every night and inhaled his intoxicating scent once again. The memories filled me and made me want to make more. I finally put the pillow back on the bed and went to the bathroom door. The shower water still ran so I undressed before I opened it. I walked in and saw his silhouette through the steamed-up glass doors. I put my hand on one of them to push it open and when I slid it to the side, the barrel of a nine-millimeter stared back at me.

"What the fuck are you lurkin' through my shit for?" He asked before he even looked at me. I grabbed his wrist and that is when he noticed.

"It's me Brandon," I said as he lowered his gun.

He had to have known that I would come to him but I still knew that he was surprised.

Brandon pulled me into his embrace and held me tight. "I'm sorry Brandon, I'm sorry that I didn't listen to you."

"Why didn't you reach out to me? I never changed my number, It's been the same all these years."

"I couldn't have expected you to ride with me after I left you like that. I was embarrassed because I really thought Marcus would be by my side in this and he wasn't. I had no one Brandon. I did every day by myself."

He noticed my arms and pulled them out in front of me. "What the hell is all this?" He asked as he looked at the scars.

"I tried to kill myself several times. My most recent was the week before they released me. I just wanted to die. I didn't think anyone would care because no one cared the entire time I was there."

"I cared, but I had to let you make your own choices and you chose him." He said in a disappointing voice.

"Yeah, I know, I just, I felt like I owed him something and it took me all these years to realize that I didn't owe him shit. I'm gonna make him pay, though. I'm gonna make him feel my pain."

"Shhh. we ain't gonna talk about him right now, let's just enjoy this moment."

Brandon slid the shower door shut and started to kiss me. His tongue ignited my insides and I fell right back in sync with him. It had been so long since I had felt such ecstasy. He kissed each and every part of my body and reminded me of all the reasons I had run straight to him. When we were done, we went down to the kitchen where he prepared me a meal fit for a queen. There were things I needed to know, so I asked.

"Why did you stop dealing with Marcus?"

He raised his eyebrows and said, "there was no way I could keep dealing with him after he let you go through with that bullshit charge you took. He reached out but I made up a lie. I told him that I was shutting down the shop because shit had gotten hot. I told him that I was going to Colombia for a few months to put in some work with one of the cartels that my father used to run with. Told him I'd hit him up when I came back. Then I waited about a month and a half and had Jambo contact him and tell him I got murked coming out of Colombia. The nigga tried to get Jam to put him on but Jam told him that I didn't leave any product behind and he didn't know how to reach out to my connect. Fuck, nigga offered him a job but my boy hung up on him and we never heard from Marcus again."

"So who is his supplier now?"

"He's been dealing with Echo and his crew. Got some shit coming out of Brooklyn where the girl's people are at. Swag be making them runs to the BK to pick up."

I thought for a minute and came up with an idea, "I think me and Swag need to meet up."

Brandon looked at me crazy and asked, "Why? You should just let that shit go. What's done is done and no matter what you do, you can't change it. I lost you for over ten years and I'm not trying to lose you again."

"I have to make him feel my pain or I will never rest. I took a fucking murder charge for his selfish ass and saved him from spending the rest of his life in prison. That bastard left me for dead and he owes me. I want that debt paid Brandon and you can either stick in there with me and help me or I can go and do it on my own. Your choice," I stated with an attitude.

"Help you huh? If you were any other bitch giving me an ultimatum, I would send you packin' and tell you to kiss my ass."

I smiled and said, "well then, I guess I'm glad that I'm not just any other bitch."

He pushed the plate of food in front of me and said, "eat and get full and we'll go from there."

I picked up my fork and ate the T-bone steak that was in front of me. It seemed to melt in my mouth and I savored each and every bite. The ketchup-covered french fries were crispy and perfect. Brandon was the total package and I wish that I would have chosen him over Marcus all those years ago. I stopped mid-bite and stated, "I called you."

He looked at me crazy and asked, "what the hell are you talking about?"

"I called you Brandon. The day I walked into the courtroom. I just needed to hear your voice. If I would have heard your voice on the other end, I never would have gone through with it but you didn't answer, a woman did."

Brandon looked confused. "A woman?" Nah, I ain't never allowed a female to answer my shit. You must have dialed the wrong number or something. I don't even bring females over here." I shook my head and replied, "no Brandon, it was the right number. I know what I dialed and hearing that woman's voice helped me make my decision. If only you would have answered instead, I never would have chosen him."

He was quiet for a minute as if he had to think about what I said, and then he spoke, "wait a minute, there was a female here that day but I don't remember her answering the phone. I was angry about her presence so I wasn't really in my right state of mind. She must have heard my phone ring and answered it."

"Who Brandon? Who was here with you?"

"Nah, she wasn't with me. She was with my boy Jambo. She just showed up at the door and thought she was gonna stay. She was running from her pops and came here but she came to the wrong place. I told Jam that he had to take her somewhere else if he wanted to keep her. She must have answered my phone."

"Tell me who it was B. I need to know."

"It was Carrie. It had to be. You know that you are the only female I have ever let up in my shit, but she knew where I lived from coming here with you. Her dad banned her from the hood and threatened to take out all the niggas she hung around. Nobody really wanted to fuck with her after that because they ain't want the heat, so she packed up and came up here. She's been with Jam ever since."

I knew that Brandon was telling me the truth. I don't think he had it in him to lie to me, so I believe him. I knew that Carrie would one day find her way back here and for all these years, I thought it was for him. I was relieved to find out she came back for Jambo. When I called Brandon's phone that day, I recognized her voice but I just needed him to tell me. I had to hear it from his mouth.

I kept quiet and then began to eat the rest of my food, but listened while Brandon spoke. "I'm retiring from the game. I told myself that I would ball and make as much money as I could until your release date."

"Why my release date?"

"I wanted to be free of everything just in case you came back to me. I didn't want anything to jeopardize my future with you. But now I got to worry about losing you to Marcus all over again because you are on some get back shit."

I got up from the bar stool I had sat on to eat and walked around the kitchen island to get to him. He turned and faced me and when he did, I said, "Brandon, you are not going to lose me to Marcus again. I know you really don't understand why I'm doing it but you're not the one who suffered for over ten years because of him."

He pulled away from me and exclaimed, "What the fuck do you mean I didn't suffer, I was in love with you and you ran to him instead of staying with me and look what happened. Every day that you were gone was torture. The thought of losing you again just doesn't sit right with me. I can't go through that shit again and I already know that no matter what I say, you gonna do

47

what you wanna do. I can't let you do that shit by yourself, just promise me that you won't go backwards."

"I give you my word Brandon. Those old feelings I used to have for him are gone. I'm coming home to you for the rest of my life." I kissed him and as soon as our lips connected, his phone rang.

He pulled it out of his pocket and answered, "sup Jam?"

Brandon pointed to the small television set that was in the kitchen and I turned it on only to see my face looking back at me. I turned back and looked at him with wide eyes.

"Thanks man, good lookin' out," he stated to the person on the other end of the phone and then hung up.

"Jam was just letting me know that the story about your release was being aired, which means if we see it, so does Marcus."

I pursed my lips together and then asked him "Do you think he's expecting me to show back up?"

Brandon shook his head and replied, "nah, he knows you don't have shit to go back to and everyone who was attached to Feelow is going to be looking at you sideways. He knows you'll be a target so he doesn't think you'll pop up."

"So what do I do now?" I asked.

Brandon smiled at me and then told me the plan.

***

"Damn nigga, where the hell you been at?" Swag asked me as soon as I walked into the house. Him and Echo had two naked hoes making out on the couch in front of them.

"Come on in and chill dawg. We rolled up some kush and got a show going on. Shit, these hoes 'bout to turn up," Echo said with a smile on his face and a drink in his hand.

"Nah man, I'm good. I'm about to pull back out in a few anyway," I said and walked to the back room of the house. A couple of minutes later, I heard someone walk into the room behind me. I turned around and stared Echo in the eyes, "Aye Tag, you good my man?" He asked me in a concerned voice.

"Yeah dawg, I'm straight. Just came to grab a couple of things and then I got to make another run," I replied.

"You handle that shit for Marcus?"

I didn't respond to his question because Echo was my boy and the last thing I wanted to do was disappoint him and lie. However, he knew me better than anybody and even without a response, he knew the answer.

"Ah Tag, what the fuck man? What the hell happened? You ain't never been unsuccessful on a caper. Did something go wrong?"

I sat down on the edge of the bed and rested my elbows on my knees and folded my hands together. I looked up at my best friend and said, "I couldn't do it E. I had every intention of knocking that bitch off but when I picked her up, she reminded me so much of Carla that I couldn't go through with it."

"Damn Tag, what the hell is it with you and them crackheads? Them mutha fuckas ain't no longer good for nothing once they get hooked on that shit. They spend all their time smoking their life away. They don't mean you no good man, especially them damn hoes. Them crack hoes done been ran through by everybody on the block. That pussy ain't no more good, so what the hell are you gonna do with it?"

I looked at him and replied, "man, when my pops got murdered, my momma couldn't cope and turned to that shit to cool up the pain so it wouldn't hurt so bad. She went from a Nubian queen to a peasant in a matter of months. The whole block lost respect for her and when she went around looking for a fix, they made her do unimaginable things to get it. Nobody tried to help her, they just fed her that poison and used her up like trash. I was too young to understand what that shit did to a person and too embarrassed to speak up. My mom came in one night looking defeated because that shit had gotten the best of her and when I looked at her, I noticed what I had been missing for a while. I saw a broken heart that was trying to mend itself back together. I could see the queen she was before and it changed my whole outlook. I wanted to help her but I just didn't know where to begin. That's when I started robbin' niggas, the same ones that treated her like shit. I'd get it and bring it back to her so she never had to leave the house but it still wasn't enough. It's easy for me to kill a man and even a woman if they deserve it but when they are on that shit, I can't pull the trigger because I see my momma looking back at me."

"So how did your moms end up dying?" What happened man?" Echo asked.

I thought back to the day it happened and hung my head low.

"Please. I promise I'll pay you your money but I gotta buy food to feed my son first."

"Fuck you and your son bitch. I want my damn money today." The dealer exclaimed and pulled the gun out of his waistband. He put it to her head and stated, "I tell you what you can do. Take them damn clothes off and pay me another way."

"I, I can't do it like that. My son, my son just walked in. Please!" She pleaded.

The dealer turned and looked behind him and it only fueled his rage even more. "Take that shit off like I said. He gonna have to see some pussy one day. Might as well start with his momma's."

She looked at me with tears in her eyes and said, "I'm sorry Terrance. Please forgive me."

The dealer walked over to me and grabbed my arm and pulled me into the bedroom where he had my momma down on her knees. "Sit your ass on that bed and don't fucking move. If you do, it will be her blood on your hands, and make sure you watch."

I tried not to cry because I knew that would hurt my mother even more. However, I couldn't stop the flow of tears as they fell from my eyes. I had known for a while that momma was on drugs. I had sat back and watched her go from a woman with class to a woman I no longer recognized. I never once questioned her because I wanted to keep imagining her as the strong woman who had raised me. Every day, her habit had grown bigger and to the point of no return, and I made it worse when I started giving it to her. She looked at me with a fear in her eyes that I had never seen before and stood up. She tried once again to change the dealer's mind, "Please. At least send him to his room. I can't do this with him in here. Please."

The dealer then turned the gun on me. The cold tip of it pressed hard against my forehead. I wanted to jump up and attack him but I knew that there was no use. I wasn't strong enough to defend the woman I admired. "No, no please, please, I'll take them off just don't hurt him. He's my baby, please don't hurt him."

She began to take her clothes off in a furry and then dropped back to her knees. "Go ahead and pull that mutha fucka out and do what you do best," he said with a smile.

I watched as her hands shook but did as he asked. She looked at me but knew that I couldn't help her.

"Suck that mutha fucka, what the hell you waiting on bitch?" He grabbed a handful of her hair and yanked her head toward him. The tears streamed down her face as she pulled him into her mouth. "Yeah. That's what I'm talking about. This how a nigga 'pose to get his dick sucked," The man turned and looked at me and then said, "this how you handle these mutha fuckin crack heads shorty. You make these bitches submit and then they realize who is in control."

He pushed her head back some as he could fall out of her mouth and then, "bend that ass over on the bed beside ya boy."

"No, no. I won't do that. You'll have to kill me first."

He cocked the gun and said, "nah bitch, I'm a kill your bastard, not you. That lil nigga can't give me no pussy so what the fuck I'm a spare him for? You love him so much, then you better come play because he doesn't mean shit to me."

"Okay, okay. Please don't hurt him. Please."

She stood to her feet and bent over on the bed. He then got behind her but before he did anything else, he turned to me and said, "come on over here and spread those ass cheeks for me boy, hold that shit open so I can get in there."

She came up off the bed but before she could get a word out, he hit her with the butt of the gun. Blood gushed from the wound and seeped on the bed under her. I knew she may not be so lucky the next time, so I got up off the bed and did as he asked. He slid into my momma with force and it caused my hands to slip off of her. However, he was so far gone that he didn't even realize I was no longer assisting him. He pumped into her several times and then said, "I'm about to cum bitch. Come on up and swallow it for me," He pulled out of her and she turned around but instead of looking at me she closed her eyes and pulled him into her mouth once again. She almost gagged when he released his juices down her throat. When he was finally done, he put his manhood back in his pants and zipped them up.

"The next time my money don't be right, it's gonna be his ass I get in. You gonna learn not to fuck with my bread," he exclaimed and then walked out leaving me and momma in tears.

She then turned to me and said, "baby, go get your momma a towel so she can clean up."

I ran out of the room to do as she asked me and as soon as I pulled a towel out of the hallway closet, I heard a gun go off.

I was afraid to walk back into the room because deep inside, I knew what I would find. My mother lay there with a blank stare in her eyes and a hole in her temple. I ran to her side and pulled her up to me but I knew that she was gone and never coming back. I held her for hours and cried and swore that I would never walk away from an addict again without trying to help them first.

"Damn Tag, I'm sorry man. I ain't never heard that shit about your moms before. I guess now I understand but what you gonna tell Marcus 'cause he gon' ask." Echo said after I finished the story.

"I'm a tell him the job was done and that nigga int' gonna question it."

"And what you think is gonna happen when he hears about Tammy being on the block still? His ass gonna come for you and that shit gonna start a fucking war."

"Look, I'm about to go pick Tammy back up and take her somewhere safe until this shit blows over."

"Tag, this shit ain't gonna 'eva blow over. That bitch was a witness to a murder that Marcus committed and let someone else take the fall for. She ain't gon' never be able to resurface 'cause if she does, that nigga gonna kill her anyway and then he's coming for your ass." Echo stated with anger in his voice.

I looked up at him but said nothing. I got up off the bed and started to pack a small bag. I didn't want to hear any other shit else he had to say; my mind was made up and I wasn't about to let him change it.

"Dammit Tag, does that crackhead mean that fucking much?"

I turned around and ran up to him pushing him against the wall. I grabbed a fist full of his shirt and answered his question.

"Just because they are on that shit doesn't mean that they ain't worth something nigga, I lost my fucking momma because of that shit. She blew her fucking brains out because of it. I couldn't do a fucking thing to help her. So yeah, that crackhead does mean that much and I'm not gonna walk away and turn my back to this one like I did Carla and my momma, and if you got a problem with that, then you can kiss my ass," I let him go and grabbed the bag I had packed and walked out leaving him to make some sense out of what I was about to do.

Corey Robinson

Chapter Five

"Yo Swag, you ready to make that trip?" Echo asked me as he kicked the chair I had fallen asleep in. I thought that I was dreaming at first but when I felt his kick on the chair again, I opened my eyes.

"Damn, can a bitch get a couple more hours of sleep first? Tetris ass ain't going nowhere."

Tetris was my uncle and the biggest cocaine and heroin supplier in all of New York. I never went outside the family to cop my packages even if prices were cheaper elsewhere. My uncle had been in the game for as long as I could remember and he was very punctual when it came to his business. He liked for all his business to be handled by time. I've seen mutha fuckas being late before and they paid for it with their life. He always felt that not being on time meant that they were up to something else other than his business, and he didn't like the thought of that.

"Nah bitch, you can't get a couple more hours because you know your uncle be trippin'. Besides, Marcus already had plans for the shipment, so he has deadlines to meet. We can't afford no setbacks right now. We are on top and one slip up will knock us back down, so get your big butch-lookin' ass up and go get ready to make that pick up."

"Aight, aight. Shit, a bitch can't neva relax around here. Mutha fucka." I exclaimed and got up from the chair so I could jump in the shower and prepare for the trip. I noticed that Tag wasn't in the house and wondered where he was. "Yo Echo, where the hell is Tag at? It don't never take him that damn long to knock a bitch off, what's up with that?"

Echo came back into the room and looked at me funny and stated, "just know that he'll be back. He had to take care of some extra shit."

I could read Echo's expression and that alone told me what had gone down. "Ah hell no, don't tell me that nigga pulled back and spared the bitch. What the hell is wrong with him." Man, Marcus gonna come for his ass if he finds out."

"Aye, you know Tag, he ain't gonna let Marcus find out shit. That nigga's heart might not make much sense but his mind knows what to do. We gonna have his back no matter what. Even when his decisions don't seem right, we still gotta be on point with everything though, so that way don't nothing seems off. That's why you need to go ahead and get your shit together so you can get on that road. You know your uncle gon' trip if you don't show up on time."

"Yeah dawg, I'm a go get ready and head out," I said and went to prepare for my ride to Brooklyn.

I couldn't believe what Echo had said about Toe Tag. He was always on point but now, another crackhead had knocked him off balance. I didn't like the sound of it and if I had to do the job myself, I would because I knew that Marcus would come for him if he finds out. I planned on having Tag's back at all costs even if it cost me my life.

***

"Come on lil nigga, get your ass in the car so I can take you home, and don't run off on your momma like that again, especially when you are talking about killing a bitch."

I could hear everything my uncle Marcus was telling me but I wasn't listening. So that shit went in one ear and out the other. All I could think about was the conversation with my momma and him. I hoped that I was wrong about how I felt but my gut was telling me different. I got in the car and slammed the door behind me. I was gonna talk to my momma and see how she felt about uncle Marcus' answer and if she was good with it, I'd leave that shit alone and focus back on the white girl.

On the drive home, I could feel him every time he turned his head to look at me. "Yo, Khalif, you good son?" He finally asked.

I didn't turn my head and look at him but I gave him an answer, "I ain't yo' son man. I'm Feelow's seed and don't ever forget that."

The car suddenly slowed down and he pulled over to the side of it and exclaimed, "mutha fucka, let me tell you something, I don't know what the hell our damn problem is but you better get your weight up before you come at me sideways. You better realize who the fuck you talking to because I may not be your daddy but I'll beat your ass like one. You understand?"

When I didn't answer him, he punched me in the arm and said, "lil nigga, answer my fuckin' question."

I turned my head and looked him in the eyes and responded, "Yeah, I understand but make that the last time you put your fucking hands on me."

"Aight, as long as you stay in your place, we won't have any more problems."

He put the car back in gear and drove me home. I thought that he would just drop me off but his black ass cut the engine and got out with me. I knew that he was going inside so he could relay to my momma what went down between us. So when she opened the door, I shot straight to my room.

"Oh Marcus, thank you so much for bringing him home. I have been so worried about him, especially with all that shit he's been talking."

"Yeah, that lil nigga gonna be alright but, for some reason, he is coming at me sideways. He overheard our conversation earlier and called himself questioning me. I'm telling you Keisha, you need to keep that lil mutha fucka on lock before he becomes a product."

I stood at the door of my room and listened to what all uncle Marcus had said but it didn't mean shit to me. My momma idolized him and when I heard them go into her bedroom, I knew exactly what was up. I couldn't believe that she was being disloyal to my daddy. I mean, I know that she got lonely at times but she could at least find someone who wasn't affiliated with my pops like that. How could she disrespect his memory? I planned on keeping an ear out because something wasn't right about my uncle

Marcus. I was no longer focused on killing the white girl. Instead, if she resurfaced, I was going to get her to tell me the truth so I could hit the right target and when I did, I didn't plan on missing.

***

I was so happy to see Carrie again and she seemed to be perfect for Jambo. Carrie was about that life, so I knew that he was in good hands. We all met up at Brandon's condo so we could work out the details of what we needed to do for the night we robbed Swag.

"Aight, I got this homeboy I used to go to school with. This white boy is a straight-up gangsta too. Owes me a favor from back in the day, so I'm gonna cash in," Brandon explained.

"He's a moonshine runner named Jeffrey Buford. Uses his club to filter the money coming in from the shine."

"And how exactly is that going to help us set up the robbery?" I asked.

"Swag frequents the club. Goes there every time she comes back from a run. Echo doesn't even have a clue. If he found out, he'd be pissed. Buford is going to let Carrie pose as one of the dancers. Said Swag usually asks him to pick out the best one and he's going to give her Carrie." Brandon turned to Carrie and said, "Make sure you give that bitch a nice and slow performance. Give me and Kry's time to pull the drugs out. Jambo's gonna keep watch."

"And how are we going to know where the drugs are in the vehicle? Don't you think that information is imperative to pull this off? Shouldn't we wait for Swag to come out of the club and get her before she pulls out?" I asked curiously.

Brandon replied, "Hell naw, we don't need no information from that bitch. I already know where the stash is at. Baby, I've been in this business since I was a jit and there ain't a nigga alive that can hide shit from me. We are going straight to the product and once we clean it out, I'm a send a text to Buford so he can pull Carrie out. By the time Swag comes outta the club, we gon' be long gone. She ain't even gonna know the spot is empty until she gets to Marcus and opens up."

"My nigga, you know I'm ready to do this. Fuck ass mutha fuckas ain't gonna know what hit 'em," Jambo exclaimed and pulled Carrie into an embrace.

Brandon looked at Carrie and asked, "Aye, you feel good about pulling this off?"

She smiled and replied, "hell yeah, I feel good about it. Marcus is going to pay for every year my girl sat in that dungeon. He deserves everything that he is going to get."

Jambo pulled out a joint and passed it to Carrie to light up. When they started passing it, a knock came at the door, so I decided to get up and answer it. "I got it baby but make sure you save me a pull of that." I walked out of the living room and into the foyer so I could see who was showing up to Brandon's condo unannounced, and when I opened the door, drama stared back at me.

"Bitch, who the hell are you and why are you answering my man's door?" the woman on the other side of the door asked.

She was pretty in her own way and had the body of an exotic dancer. I looked her up and down and gave her a smile to let her know that she didn't faze me. I figured she had to be one of the many bitches that Brandon had fucked with while I was away. I couldn't blame him though because if I was gay, I would have fucked with the bitch too.

"Um, do you mind telling me who you're looking for because the only man that lives here is mine?" I said with a sarcastic look on my face.

The bitch didn't answer me but instead stormed past me like she was running things. I shut the door behind her and shrugged my shoulders as if her presence didn't bother me. However, I was a woman scorned and if the bitch came looking for it, I wasn't above giving her what she asked for.

***

When I knocked on the door of the condo, I expected Brandon to answer. I felt bad about the way I took off and wanted to give it one more shot but when the door opened and I saw the white girl, my whole world was shattered. Something in my heart told me that I was looking at the woman whose name he had called while I was giving him head. I knew one thing though, I was not about to answer to the bitch. I looked her in the eyes and stormed inside past her.

"Brandon, where the hell are you? I don't know who the hell …" I shouted while I made my way to the living room but when I walked in and saw Jambo and his girlfriend, I shut the hell up.

"Mya, what the hell are you doing here? I keep telling your dumb ass to call before you show up over here."

"Dumb? Mutha fucka did you just call me dumb?" I asked because I couldn't believe that he would disrespect me like that in front of everyone. "Nigga, my ass wasn't dumb when you were between these thighs but now I'm dumb? Fuck you Brandon with your no-good ass. That stupid white bitch can have you."

I turned around and started to walk out but he grabbed my arm and turned me back around. "Let me tell you something Mya, and you better listen good. Don't you ever fix your mouth to disrespect her again. Do I make myself clear?"

I looked at him with a look of fear and pain mixed together in my eyes. I was on the verge of tears but I refused to let them see me cry, I would have rather died. I stared him down but didn't answer and then the woman who had opened the door spoke.

"Hi Mya. My name is Krystal and I just wanted to thank you for holding my man down while I was away. However, I'm home now, so your services will no longer be needed. You can see yourself out."

I looked around the room at all the eyes staring back at me and felt defeated. I had held Brandon down for years and really thought that we would have a future together. My heart was shattered into tiny pieces and I could only hope to put it back together.

I looked at the white girl and stated, "So you're Krystal? Well, where the hell have you been all this time while I was with him?" She stepped up close enough to me that I could feel her breath on my skin when she talked. She exclaimed, "Bitch, I was doing time in prison for killing a mutha fucka that tried me about my man"

"I hope you don't think that is supposed to scare me because I am not scared of you," I stated but deep down, my heart pumped rapidly.

"Oh honey, I don't want you to be scared, I want you to be careful because I don't play about my territory. So, unless you have some questions for me, you can leave."

I stared into her eyes and if looks could kill, she would be dead. I felt so humiliated. He had never even let on that he had a woman in his life. When I was giving him head that night and he called her name, it was the first time he'd mentioned her. The bitch may have meant something to him but to me, I could have cared less about her. I turned around to face him so I could ask him one last thing but I never got the question out of my mouth.

The white girl said, "Nah bitch, he ain't got no answers for you, so you can save that shit."

My nose flared in anger and I knew that there was no use in just standing there because I was outnumbered and didn't stand a chance. I looked around the room at everyone one last time and then locked eyes with Brandon and said, "you will not get away with treating me like this. Karma is a mutha fucka and you will get yours, mark my words," and then I turned around and walked out to go plan my revenge.

***

After packing a small bag with supplies, I headed back to the hotel that I'd put Tammy up in. I only hoped that she was still there. I hadn't told her yet that I picked her up to kill her but planned on having that conversation hoping that it would make her stay in. If I spared her and let her live, when Marcus finds out, he would not only be after her, but he'd be after me too.

I wasn't trying to bring any heat to the camp, so I needed to convince Tammy to stay put for a while.

I knocked on the hotel room door when I arrived and got nervous when it wasn't answered right away, "dammit, I knew I should have taken the key," I said to myself. I waited another minute and then turned around to leave but before I took two steps, I heard the door being unlocked.

"I'm sorry, I was in the shower. It felt so good I didn't want to come out." Tammy stated while she stood at the door with nothing on but a towel wrapped around her. The beads of shower water were still on her mocha-colored skin. My dick hardened at the sight of her beauty that others hadn't seen in a while.

"You thought I dipped on you?" She asked and then pursed her lips together.

"Yeah, I did. I ain't even gonna lie. I'm glad to see you're still here, though." I replied.

"Well, I won't lie either then. I thought about it but then decided that I could use some peace. Get myself together. Take a nice hot shower and who knows maybe you'll buy me lunch."

"Oh shit, yeah, I guess I should feed you huh," I said with a laugh.

"Yeah, that would be nice," she said and laughed too.

I stood there and took in each and every inch of her and when she walked up closer to me, her towel came off and my dick stood at attention. However, I didn't bring her to the hotel to trick her, but instead, to save her life. I licked my lips and said, "Aye Tammy, we need to talk about something really important before we go any further."

She gave me a look of disappointment and then bent down to pick up the towel that was at her feet. "Oh! Um okay. I'm so sorry Tag. I just thought that ... well, you know."

"It's all good, and call me Terrance. Don't worry, I'm gonna get to that pussy soon enough but I didn't bring you here to fuck you. I brought you here to save you."

She looked at me confused and asked, "what the hell are you talking about? Save me from what?"

I pointed to the bed and said, "sit down Tammy. I need you to be able to understand everything I'm about to tell you, and I also need you to trust me."

"Um okay, just let me get decent real quick," she stated and picked up the shorts and t-shirt that she'd had on when I picked her up. I told myself that I needed to make sure I picked her up some gear. After she put her clothes back on, she sat down on the bed, and said, "Okay, I'm all ears."

"Look Tammy, I don't mean to scare you or anything but I didn't pick you up for a trick. I picked you up to kill you."

As soon as I said it, she jumped up from the bed and tried to make a dash for the door but I was faster and stronger than her, so she didn't make it very far.

"No please. Please don't kill me," she pleaded with a desperate look in her eyes and then said, "I know that I'm only a dope fiend and ain't worth a shit but I'm not ready to die." I walked her back to the bed and motioned for her to sit back down and told her what I could.

"Look at me Tammy, because I need you to understand how serious this shit is. If I was really going to kill you I would have done it by now, so since you're still breathing, that means I have no intentions of harming you. However, if you don't do exactly as I tell you and stay out of the fucking streets, you're as good as gone."

Her voice cracked as she replied, "Who? Who wants me dead and why would you spare me? You don't even know me like that."

I replied, "oh, I know you, just not in the ways that I'm hoping to. But all that shit is irrelevant right now. I was hired to take your life and could get a sweet payday if I do it but I ain't thinking about that money right now."

"You mean, you get paid to kill people? But why me? I've never done anything to nobody."

Corey Robinson

"Let's just say that some years ago, you were a witness to something that could put someone away for the rest of their life, and with you dead, the problem no longer exists."

"Hmmm," she sat for a minute in deep thought and then asked, "did my cousin send you?"

"Nah, Tammy, someone more powerful sent me your way. However, I really don't want to kill you, but you have to do as I say."

"Oh yeah? Well, what is that?" She asked.

"You have to stay inside. You cannot leave this room under any circumstances unless it's with me. I'm going to find another place for you but it will be out of town. You just gotta give me a minute, though." I said.

"So you're telling me that I'm basically a prisoner right now. How the fuck do you expect me to get the things I need if I'm locked up in here? Can you answer that?"

"Don't worry, I'm going to provide everything. Clothes, food, drugs, and some good dick, but before you get that, I gotta get you checked out."

"I don't have any diseases if that's what you're checking for. I use protection with all my tricks. I smoke crack but I do still have a little bit of dignity left in me."

"Aight, we'll see about that, meanwhile, I'm gonna go grab you some food and some gear and I'll be back," I said and then pulled out a small baggie from my jeans pocket. I reached out so she could take it. She hesitated for a minute but eventually took it out of my hand. I had to keep her safe and knew the only way to keep her from leaving was to feed her habit. However, I hoped that I'd eventually be able to save her from the drugs too.

"That should hold you until I get back. Now, what size clothes do you need?" I asked her.

"You never told me why you're doing this. I need to know because you don't owe me a fuck thing and you putting yourself on the line for me is just something I'm not getting. So tell me."

"I was once in love with a woman who indulged in the things you are into. I made the mistake of dropping her back off in the same streets I'd picked her up from and I never saw her again. I also sat back and watched my momma deteriorate from that shit you are smoking, she lost sight of everything but the pipe and it ended up costing her. I won't lose someone else."

"But why do you care? What's in it for you?"

"A clean conscience, and a hope that one day maybe you'll want to give that shit up."

"You know Terrance, I haven't always been like this. I use to have it all together, but I fucked around and caught feelings for a nigga that didn't give a fuck about me. He only used me because he was trying to find out information about the woman he really wanted. He even got her pregnant and everything. Even after he did me dirty, my dumb ass still went back for more. We were together one night and I rode with him to a house he claimed his mother lived in. When she opened the door, he shot the man that stood behind her, and then he went in and closed the door. I waited in the car for what seemed like forever and when I started to get out to go in and check on him, a set of headlights appeared. I saw two people get out of the car and go in and then, they brought him out and threw him in their trunk. My instincts kicked in, so I followed them at a distance in his car and oh my god, it changed my life forever. I, I, I watched him get beaten and then he was shot in the head. I didn't know what else to do to mask the pain, so I started getting high and once I started, I couldn't stop."

Tears flowed from her eyes and I sat on the bed beside her to bring her some comfort. I couldn't believe that she had told me the details of Feelow's murder.

"It's alright now, you can start over. I'll help you but you gotta keep it real at all times. I know that shit haunts you but if you let me, I'll help you forget about it, you won't need that crackshit anymore if you'll just let me in."

She stopped crying and pulled away from me with a frightened look on her face and said, "Wait a minute. Who the hell sent you to kill me?"

I looked her in the eyes and answered her question.

Chapter Six

When I stormed out of the living room, I had every intention of leaving but something stopped me. I opened the front door and closed it back to make it sound like I'd left. I wanted to hear everything they said about me, but once I was gone, I became an afterthought to them. Apparently, they had better things to talk about and I stood there and took it all in.

"Okay, so what time are we going to show up at the club? We can't be off on our timing at all. " Krystal said.

Brandon replied, "Well, Swag will pick up the product from her uncle and leave right out after that. Tetris likes everything to run according to plan; whenever something is off it makes him paranoid."

"So she never just chills and spends time with her uncle?" Carrie asked curiously.

"Nah, not when a run is being made. She only goes to chill every few months or so and when she does, she doesn't drive a car that has compartments."

"How do you know all of this Brandon?" Krystal asked.

He replied. "My father schooled me very well. There is not a drug dealer or runner along the east coast that I don't know about. I know every move they make when it comes to their business."

"Damn dawg. Your pops was straight with that shit," Jambo exclaimed.

"Yeah, he wanted to make sure that no one could ever shake me, and so far, I haven't had any issues."

"Okay, so we show up at the club before Swag and get every-thing set up with your buddy. Carrie works the inside, Jambo watches the outside and we take the bricks. Simple as that," Krystal stated with a little excitement in her voice.

"Yep, simple as that," Brandon replied.

I had heard enough about the bullshit move they would pull. I wondered who Swag was and wished that I could warn them. I quietly opened the door so I could slip out but before I stepped out, I noticed a set of keys and an ID card on the table beside the coat rack. I reached my hand down and picked it up to see who it belonged to and noticed that it was a department of Corrections inmate ID card. I looked at the white bitch in the photo and then at the name "Krystal Madison," I said in a low voice. I pulled out my cell phone and took a photo of the card I held in my hand. I was anxious to see what I could find out about her because whatever it was, I was going to bury her with it. I sat the card back down on the table right where I got it from and walked out.

My mind was all fucked up because I didn't deserve to be dissed like that. I had thought better of Brandon because he had never disrespected me in that way. I knew there were a lot of moments where he seemed distant but never once thought it was due to another female. He never mentioned her before or anyone else, so I never had a reason to believe that his heart belonged to someone else.

I pulled into the apartment complex I lived in which was a far cry from what Brandon's condo looked like. I hinted to him for many years to let me move into his place and he always said the same thing, "Nah, let a nigga have time to miss your ass. If you live here, you gonna always be around and take the excitement I feel when you're away from me for too long and then show up." However, I now knew it was all a lie, I felt like such a fool.

I finally decided to get out of my car and walked up the stairs to my lonely dwelling. My hand shook when I tried to put the key in the lock but I was finally able to hold it steady and open the door. I threw my bag on the couch and sat down. I knew that there was no use in me feeling sorry for myself because it was Brandon's loss. I sat back for a minute and thought about my next step.

I remembered the screenshot I took of the white girl's prison ID card and pulled my phone out. I then sat up and opened my laptop that sat on the table in front of me. While it warmed up, I pulled out my compact and opened it to reveal a small bag of cocaine, a blade and a mirror. It was a habit I'd been able to keep hidden from Brandon. He never knew that I snorted powder, so I either hide it very well or he just never paid enough attention to me to even care.

I inhaled the white substance up my nose and held my head back for a second, "Ah, I needed that," I said to myself and then put the compact away. "Okay miss Krystal Madison, let's see if I can find some skeletons in our closet."

I googled the name and the only thing that came up was a newspaper article. I read it out loud as if I was reading to an audience "suspect in Feelow murder case, Marcus Newsome set free after Krystal Madison walks into courtroom and admits to crime." I raised an eyebrow and said, "so that's what she went to prison for but let's see who Mr. Newsome is, and what did he mean to her." I googled his name next and saw a photo of a handsome thug on my screen and said "Well Marcus, since I can't find out what your relationship was with her on google, then maybe I should ask you in person."

I got up and went to pack a small bag so I could make the trip to the town he lived in. I am ready to show Brandon and Krystal that they had fucked over the wrong bitch and I knew just what to say to get the dude named Marcus on my side.

***

"Aye unc, I'm sorry I'm late, some shit came up. It won't happen again," I said to my uncle Tetris as soon as I walked into the stash house. The truth was, I'd run into a shorty I'd been trying to get with for the longest and I couldn't pass up the opportunity.

Tetris looked at me with raised brows and a flared nose and said, "You being my niece doesn't give you a pass when it comes to my business dealings. I've killed mutha fuckers for being late and yet, you want me to spare you because some shit came up."

I was a little nervous after he said that but refused to show it. The last thing I needed was for Echo to find out I was behind on the run. "Ah come on unc. I ain't never been late before and I know that don't give me an excuse but I promise it won't happen again."

He got quiet and only sat there and stared at me. His body-guard stood behind me like big brown statues but they never intimidated me. Tetris was my pops brother and practically raised me, so I knew deep in my heart that he wouldn't harm me. "We've been doing this for years, and you're right, you have never been off, so how could you possibly have let a piece of pussy throw you off your game and before you deny it, I know our every move from the time you pull out of your driveway until the time you pull into mine," he finally stated.

I held my head low because I couldn't believe that he knew what had caused me to be late. That meant he knew about my stops to the club too. "I'm sorry unc, but I had been trying to get with shorty for the longest. I ain't mean no disrespect."

He nodded his head and stated, "Always remember that pussy can get a man killed. I love it just as much as you but don't let it be the death of you," he then pointed to the two duffle bags on the floor beside him and said, "boys." His bodyguards each picked a bag up and left the room. I knew they were going to pack the car I had driven. I felt a sense of relief come over me because I knew that I was off the hook but I had to make sure I didn't make the mistake again.

He looked at me and said in his deep baritone voice, "This will be your only pass."

I nodded and replied, "Yes sir, it won't happen again. I give you my word." I then turned around and walked out. I didn't think that there was another man on earth that frightened me as much as my uncle Tetris. For some reason, I took his threats more seriously than anybodys. I held a huge amount of respect for him and felt bad for my misdeed. I never wanted him to think bad of me. It was hard enough being a gay dominant female in a game where real men ruled, so I knew I always had to be a step ahead so no one could push me back.

I got outside just as the bodyguards were placing the siding back on the vehicle. Once it was sealed, they nodded and walked away. In all my years, I had never heard either one of them speak a word. I wondered if I ever would, I shrugged my shoulders and then hopped in the ride.

I usually stopped at the strip club on the way out of town but was skeptical because now that I knew Tetris kept an eye on me, it made me rethink my moves. Going to that club was a ritual and a weakness. I thought about my options and I figured since the business was taken care of, I should be good. "Fuck it," I said out loud and got on the highway so I could go to my next destination.

I had my music booming from the speakers in my trunk when I pulled up. I had never been real flashy but the bass coming from the woofers announced my presence. I let the song that had been playing finish before I got out, "Hell yeah, that was my shit right there," I said to myself with a smile. I reached back in my ride and opened the console so I could pull out the rolls of ones that I'd always kept handy just for the occasion. I couldn't wait to see which hottie Buford would hook me up with. He had always made sure I had the baddest bitch in the club.

"Sup Gutta?" I asked when I got to the door of the club. The bouncer had become familiar with my presence, so as soon as he saw me, he opened the door right away making me feel like a VIP celebrity.

I went in and walked straight to the bar and said to the bar-tender, "Sup man? Hey, could you let Buford know that I'm here and I'm feeling like I want a little cotton candy tonight?" Buford would know that I meant cotton candy. As a white girl, I tried to switch up every time. I went there because nothing was wrong with having a little flavor in your life.

The bartender picked up his phone and dialed the numbers that put him through to Buford's office. He spoke and then I listened to the response and then hung up, "Buford said go to room number four. He's got something special for you tonight." The bartender stated.

I ordered a small bottle of moonshine and got two glasses and made my way to room number four. Buford had set up six rooms in the back of his club for special customers to be able to enjoy themselves and I just so happen to be one of the special ones. I couldn't wait for the bitch to grind their pussy on my lap and the thought of it made my clit jump.

I walked into the room and sat in the chair that was in the middle of the floor. A small table sat beside it so I filled up the two small shot glasses with the shine and sat them atop it, and then I took a big swig from the bottle. No sooner than I sat the bottle down, the door opened and in walked a stick of cotton candy. She went to the CD player and popped in a disc and as soon as Beyonce's voice filled the room, she turned to me.

I looked at her lustfully and licked my lips while she dropped the robe she'd had round her. I was turned on by her blonde hair and faintly tanned skin. She wore a peach-colored bra and thong set and I was anxious for her to remove them. She swayed her hips to the music and stood in front of me.

"You gonna take that shit off and let a nigga see that fatty?" I asked and licked my lips.

She smiled and replied, "Depends on how much time you got. A girl like me doesn't wanna rush a good thing."

I ran a finger down her nicely flat stomach and stopped at the edge of her thongs and said, "Mmm, for you, I got all the time in the world, but what are you gonna show me to keep me entertained?"

She untied the back strap of her bra and flashed me her breasts. I couldn't tell if they were real or fake but I just knew that they were perfect. I reached over and picked up one of the shot glasses and handed it to her and then picked the other one up for myself. We tapped our glasses together and drank down the liquid.

As soon as she sat her glass down on the table, she sat her pretty ass on me and put on the performance of a lifetime, and right before I had a chance to slip a finger in her thong, Buford walked in and shut the party down.

***

I was nervous as fuck when I thought about the robbery on Swag. I hoped that it all went according to plan. I knew that when Swag went back to deliver Marcus his dope and it was gone he would be pissed but I could have cared less about how that bastard felt.

A few minutes after we all got in place, Swag pulled into the club's parking lot and parked. She didn't get out immediately and it made me wonder what she was doing. "Brandon, why do you think she's taking so long to get out?" I asked the man who held my heart in the palm of his hands.

"That bitch probably oiling up her clit and shit," he said with a slight chuckle.

I punched him in the arm and stated, "that is not funny," however, I still laughed.

A couple of minutes later, she got out of her car. We watched as she reached back in and pulled out what looked like rolls of paper, or better yet, money. I hoped that Carrie would take every bill Swag had in her possession because she would truly deserve it. Swag then made her way to the door and gave the bouncer some dap and then walked in.

Buford had told Brandon that when he had Swag settled in, he would send him a text. A few minutes later, Brandon's phone vibrated and the word came through, "We in there. Let's go baby."

Brandon sent a text to Jambo to let him know we were on the move so he could keep an eye out. The bouncer at the door had no clue about our presence, so we had to be careful. Brandon had told me that we would only be able to talk through hand gestures until we got back in the car.

We decided down and crept behind the four cars that were between the one we were in and Swags. When we got to her vehicle, Brandon pulled out a small metal stick and put it under the handle of the back door. He pulled and the handle popped off. He then put the stick between the window seal and the door and popped it up. He did this to each side of the back door until the outside popped off. Underneath were forty tightly compressed bricks of pure cocaine. Brandon turned his head and smiled at me.

Together, we pulled each brick out and put them in the duffle bag we had brought. When all forty were secure, Brandon placed the door cover back on and then the handle. There was no way anyone could tell that the door had ever been removed. Brandon pointed to the direction we'd come from and I turned around and led him back to our ride.

When we got in, he said, "Marcus is gonna be pissed but fuck him. That mutha fucka caused me to miss all those years of seeing you. He owes you this and much more."

I leaned over and kissed his lips and asked, "Brandon, what are we going to do with all this cocaine?"

"I'm going to sell it to Jambo for half price and give you the money, I'm outta the dope game baby but he's going to need it for his operation. These bricks along with the ones he already has are going to set him and Carrie up for life."

He pulled out his phone and texted Jambo and then Buford to let them know the job was complete. Jambo texted back and said he wasn't moving until he saw Carrie come out of the club. A couple of minutes later, we saw the white boy Buford walk Carrie out. He noticed me and Brandon and nodded. Jambo met Carrie halfway to the car and walked with her. When they both got in, Brandon backed out and pulled away leaving Swags to ride hollow.

***

"Yo Buford man, why did you pull the snow bunny out before she finished? Shit, she was just about to come outta those thongs." I asked. I was pissed because I was certain lil mama was gonna let me taste her creamy vanilla center.

"Sorry about that Swag but she had a family emergency at home. I can put someone else in there with you though. Just pick anyone you like."

I shook my head in disappointment and said, "Nah man we're good. I gotta get my ass back on the road anyway, maybe next time I come through, you could hook me up with two instead."

"Yeah man, I got you. It's always a pleasure having your business." Buford held his hand out for me to shake. I shook it and said, "Thanks. I'll be back really soon."

I went back to the bar before I left and purchased another pint of Moonshine to take back home with me and then walked out. When I got outside, my gut told me that something felt off. I stood there for a minute but when I didn't see anything strange, I shrugged my shoulders and hopped in the ride. I knew that Echo would be waiting on me so we could get the dope to Marcus, so I started the car and got back on the road.

***

"Yeah, speak to me," I said when my phone buzzed.

"Yo, that's taken care of, you should be good now," Toe Tag stated from the other end of the line and then hung up.

A big sense of relief fell over me. I was glad that I didn't have to worry about Tammy anymore and could continue living my life. I pulled up in Trap and Creep's driveway and got out. They were sitting on the porch smoking a blunt when I walked up the steps.

"Sup Marcus? You want a hit of this shit?" Creep asked but I didn't feel like getting my smoke on at that moment.

"Nah Creep, a nigga just chillin' today," I replied.

Creep shrugged his shoulders and said, "Shit, that's just more for me."

I shook my head and then said to Trap, "Aye man, I'm just stopping by to let yall know I'll be bringing some re-up by later on. Swag should be back with the shipment soon."

"Damn right man, and it'll be right on time. You know we can't afford to run out because right now, we got shit on lock." Trap replied.

"Yeah, and that's how we're going to keep it."

I sat down in the only empty chair left on the porch and no sooner than I did, Keisha pulled up. When she got out of the car, my dick instantly rocked up. Keisha had always been fine but after having Khalif, her hips spread a little wider. I adjusted my hard-on while she walked up the steps.

She asked, "Hey, have yall seen my cousin around any-where?"

"Nah, not since yall bitches got into it the other day but I'll tell you what I have seen … These mutha fuckin nuts in your mouth," Creep replied and grabbed his nut sack.

"Fuck you Creep, you'll never get this pussy," she said.

"Nigga you foul as fuck," I stated and then said to Keisha, "I ain't think you and Tammy got along, so why you looking for her?"

I thought about the conversation I and Keisha had in front of my house and wondered if she was looking for Tammy so she could try and find out if she was telling the truth or not. Little did she know, Tammy was maggot food by now.

"I just need to talk to her about something Marcus, and it ain't got shit to do with you."

"Oh yeah? With that slick-ass mouth. You wanna come in and let me put something in that mutha fucka to shut you up?" I said to her with a serious look in my eyes.

"Nah, I think I've drunk enough of your cum to last me anoth-er ten years."

"Whoa shit. Damn my nigga, you shooting like that?" Creep exclaimed.

I smiled and said "Nigga, these nuts stay full and ready to shoot at all times. Anyway, what the fuck are you trying to find your cousin for?"

She responded with an attitude, "Didn't I tell you it doesn't have shit to do with you, so why are you worried Marcus? I and you are good and that should be your only concern."

I nodded my head and said "Yeah alright. I hear what you are saying but don't let me find out you feeding that bullshit she told you about."

"Whatever Marcus, I'll catch yall later. If yall happen to see her, please tell her to call me. Marcus has the number." Keisha then turned and walked back to her car and once she got in, she looked at me through the windshield with curious eyes. I knew that she was trying to dig into that information Tammy had given her but if she wanted to question her more, then she'd have to meet that bitch in hell.

Creep broke me from my thoughts, "Dawg, you still hittin' that pussy because she actin' like you ain't slanging that dick right."

"Man, fuck Keisha. That pussy will always be mine whenever I want it and that shit ain't gonna never change." I replied confidently.

"Aye man, you heard anything about the white girl getting released? From what I understand, her time should be up. Ain't you worried about that?" Trap questioned.

I thought about what he'd asked me and then answered, "Man, I ain't worried about that cracker. That was her dumb ass that walked into that courtroom and took that charge. She'd be stupid as a mutha fucka to bring her white ass back here."

"Damn nigga, why you dissin' her like that? Shit, if it wasn't for her, your black ass would be behind those fences as we speak, shit, your ass should be grateful," Creep said and then took one last hit of the joint. He put the roach in an empty beer can and got up and went inside leaving me and Trap to ourselves.

"That mutha fucka may not always make sense but he does have a point dawg. Your ass should be grateful to that chick man, you should have ridden with that bitch till the end."

I thought about Krystal and all she had sacrificed for me and then replied, "I'm grateful Trap. I know that she could have just walked away and let me go to prison but she didn't. She stood tall just like I taught her to do. She gave up everything just so I didn't have to. I appreciate it but I had to move on with my life. I ain't worrying about her now and she probably ain't worrying about me either."

"Yeah aight, but what's your ass gonna do if she shows up on your doorstep? Killi gonna go fucking ham on that ass. You know that you were all she had."

I looked at Trap and said, "I'll worry about that when the time comes but I'm telling you, I don't think her cracker ass is coming this way." I stood up and pulled my keys out of my pocket and said, "Aye man, I got to get up out of here. I got to go meet up with Echo and Swag so I can pick up that re-up but I'll be back though."

I gave Trap some dap and walked off the porch. As soon as I got into my ride, my cell phone rang. I picked it up and checked to see who the caller was but didn't recognize the number, so I sent that shit to voicemail. Talking about Krystal had me in a fucked up mood and I didn't want to listen to anybody else's bullshit. I backed out of the driveway and headed to the stash house so I could meet up with Echo and Swag. Whoever had tried to call would have to catch up with me later because I had more important shit to deal with.

***

I finally got an address and phone number for Marcus Newsome. It had cost me a small sum of money but I knew that it would all be worth it in the end.

When I called the number, it went straight to voicemail. "Dammit, I didn't come all of this way to talk to a fucking recording," I said and threw my phone on the bed. I began to bite my nails, a bad habit I had acquired as a teenager, whenever I got nervous. Something inside of me willed me to keep going, so I picked up my phone and tried the number again.

"Yo, this Marcus. As you can hear, I am not available, so if it's that important, leave a message and I'll get back at'cha. Peace."

Hearing his voice in that message gave me some motivation, so instead of getting angry about him not answering, I decided to leave a message.

"Hello Mr. Newsome, you don't know me but my name is Mya Lopez and I'm just calling to hopefully find out some information on an ex-acquaintance of yours by the name of Krystal Madison. I'm sure we would have an uninteresting conversation, so when you find the time, please get back to me at 717-220-1431 or you can come by the Marriott Resort on lake street Room 318. I look forward to hearing from you."

I threw my phone back down on the bed and then fell on the bed beside it. I was exhausted and decided to try and get some rest. I hoped that when I woke up I would have a response from Mr. Marcus Newsome. If not, I would continue to try until he finally just answers, I couldn't wait to find out everything that went down with the murder that Krystal had gone to prison for.

I had hoped to get Brandon to see her for who she really was because I had a feeling that he only knew bits and pieces of her past. I was going to give him a history because I was sure that he would leave her and come back to me. That bitch didn't deserve him. I did and I was going to stop at nothing to get him back. I just hoped all of my hard work paid off. I got comfortable and started to drift off to sleep and right before my eyes completely shut, my cell phone rang.

Corey Robinson

Chapter Seven

As soon as my cell rant, I answered it. "Sup? Where the hell are you at? Your ass should have been back." I said angrily as soon as I put it to my ear.

"Yo Echo, nigga, I'm a be pulling up to the house in about ten minutes. I ran into a little problem on the way but I'll be there. Just make sure you and Marcus are at the house." Swag replied.

She didn't think that I knew about her little habit of stopping at the strip club before heading back. I had just never said anything to her because it had never really been an issue. Her making a pit stop might have been a good thing because if the pigs were hip to her, they'd think she would go straight back so that little stop would throw them off.

I replied, "bitch, I'm already here and Marcus should be here shortly but your ass needs to come on. I know about your little visits to the club, so don't come here and try to feed me no lies."

I could tell there was a little hesitation in her voice. She'd been busted and had no idea how to respond, "Echo man, I'm sorry dawg, but it ain't never got in the way of my business."

"Yeah, until now, you stayed in there a little longer than you should have but Marcus is running a little behind too. Just get your ass here as soon as you can," I stated and then hung up on her ass.

I wasn't about that bullshit when it came to my business and ever since Marcus has been getting his product from me, my money has doubled. I didn't want anything to veer Marcus in another direction. I used to be his competition but ever since we made amends, it's all been sweet. I became his supplier years ago after his other one cut him off and I wanted to keep my position.

Marcus had asked several times for Swag to hook him up with her uncle but Tetris wouldn't even allow me to do a pickup so I knew that Marcus was out of luck. I had sat in front of the television to catch a Hawks game when I heard the car horn blow. I got up and looked out the window and saw Marcus and stepped out the front door to let him know he was welcome.

"Aye man, come on in. Swag will be here in a few. The stupid bitch ran into some pussy on the way back and now her ass is behind.

"Shit, ain't nothing wrong with a little pussy. I think we both know how that shit puts a nigga off track," he stated with a smile. He had actually taken the news more chill than I thought he would and that brought me some relief.

I asked, "So you cool with the drop being a little off track? That ain't like you man. Your ass usually is tripping like a mutha fucka." I wondered what had him so at ease but I wasn't about to pry. "Hell, yeah. Nigga you see that dunk. Shit, Golden State can hang that fuckin' title up because it's the Hawks' time to shine." I said excitedly when the Hawks took the lead.

"Oh yeah, let's put some money on that big talkin' you doing," Marcus said.

I had never been scared to put my money on something I believed in, so I replied, aight, chump. Five G's says A-T-L get the championship title. Can you afford that lil nigga?"

"Shit, can I afford it? I say we double it to an even ten. You scared."

"Hell nah, I ain't scared, I just want you to make sure you got my 10 g's on deck as soon as the last buzzer sounds," I exclaimed.

"Bet that my man but don't be begging me to give you a few days to come up with the money once you lose, because I'ma want my shit straight up." He said with a serious look on his face.

We stopped talking shit and focused on the game, each team had already won three games and the game that showed would be the tie breaker; one of us would be ten thousand dollars richer before the end of the night. We were so into the playoffs that we didn't even hear Swag drive up in the yard.

"Damn, you niggas need to turn that shit off. I could have been anybody walking up in this mutha fucka," she said when she entered the house.

"Nah, a mutha fucka ain't that damn bold to walk up in this bitch. Fuck around and get they wig split," I said and we all shared a laugh.

Swag asked, "Aye yall ready to pull this shit out and handle business?"

Marcus answered her question but never took his focus off the screen. There were only two minutes left in the game and the score was tied. "Just give us a minute, a nigga got ten stacks riding on this bitch."

Steph Curry had control of the ball and when he jumped up to make a shot, it was knocked out of his hand and picked up by a Hawks player who then dribbled it to the other end of the court and topped the game off with a three-pointer. As soon as the timer buzzed, I held my hand out and said, "pay up bitch."

Marcus stood up from the chair he had sat in and said, "yeah, yeah, yeah. I got you man. Shit, I ain't see that coming." He then looked at Swag and stated, "aight, let's go move the product."

I got up and followed behind Swag and Marcus to the garage where Swag had parked the car. I picked up the pry bar that I used to pop the exterior off and went to the back door of the vehicle. Marcus rubbed his hands together in anticipation of the forty bricks he'd ordered.

"Damn Echo, it ain't never took you this long to pop the door. What's up man?" asked Swag with raised brows.

I replied, "I don't know man, this shit seems off track or some-thing. Shit ain't never been this hard to remove," At about that time, the door finally pulled away and I removed the siding, but when I did, there wasn't shit inside.

I looked at Swag crazy and asked, "what's up bitch? Is this some kind of fucking joke? Where the shit at?"

"What? Nigga, don't fucking play with me, that shit is ..." She exclaimed and came up on the side of the car that I was on. She stopped her words short when she saw that the compartment was empty.

Marcus asked, "what the hell is going on here? Are you sure you opened the right compartment? Maybe it's on the other side."

"Nah man, I'm on the right side but this shit is empty," I said in a disappointed voice. I held my head down and gave some thought to what was going on.

Swag exclaimed, "I'm telling you that shit was in there, uncle Tetris don't play those types of fucking games. I don't understand man. I came straight back with the exception of that one-stop but I …" she stopped talking and thought for a minute and shook her head and said, "man, I stayed in the club a little longer than usual. My boy hooked me up with a new dancer. Snow was bad as fuck too but ain't no way it could have happened at the club."

I stood up from the side of the vehicle and said, "Swag, you stop at that same club every time you go up that way. Are you sure you ain't never been followed or something? You sure that's the only stop you made? Mutha fucka, who's gonna pay for that shit? Your uncle ain't gonna wanna hear no bullshit about you getting robbed."

About that time, Marcus' cell rang. He looked at who the caller was and said, "Aye man, I 'don't know who the hell keeps calling me from this number but I'm about to find the fuck out," he then answered the vibrating phone.

Me and Swag continued to debate about the missing drugs. It made me wonder if she had been set up but the question was, by who. I kicked the side of the car and looked at Swag angrily and stated, "Aight man, we gon' have to either let your uncle know or pretend the shit never happened. As long as we come up with the bread to pay him, he'll never know but we gonna have to come up with that shit in a normal time manner so he doesn't figure out that something is off."

"Yeah, yeah I agree. I'm sorry Echo, man, I ain't see nothing unusual or anything, I swear. I would have noticed."

Marcus hung up from whomever he had talked to and had a crazy look in his eyes. His nose flared and he said, "yo, that was some bitch named Mya Lopez. Said she ran across my name when she was trying to find out information on someone else. She wants to meet up with me. Said I might appreciate what she has to tell me."

I looked at him confused and said "Mya Lopez, you know who that is man? You gonna fall for that shit."

He looked from me to Swag and stated, "bitch said she overheard some people talking about a jack, and I got a feeling the one she's talking about and the one on Swag are the same, and there's only one way to find out."

"Yo, you need me to go with you? What if you run into some bullshit. You don't know the bitch, so it could be a setup. You can't go in blind," I said, but I already knew what his answer would be.

***

I was so glad that Marcus had finally answered my call. I just hoped that he would believe me when I told him what had gone on.

I was hesitant to speak when he first came on the line but knew I had to get it over with so I said, "Hello, Marcus Newsome. I know you don't know me but my name is Mya Lopez and I have to talk to you."

"The fuck do you need to talk to me for? Do you know who the fuck I am?" He asked angrily.

I sighed and replied, "no, I don't know you. I googled your name when I saw it in an article about someone's murder."

"The hell you looking up old shit for. Bitch, I'm about to hang the fuck up if you don't tell me what the fuck you want."

I didn't want to say too much over the phone so I asked him, "Can we meet up? I sent you my hotel information earlier, maybe you could stop by. We can meet in the lobby if that makes you more comfortable."

"Give me one good reason why I should meet you anywhere."

"Well Marcus, not only am I a very attractive woman but I'm also a very knowledgeable one and I think the information I have about a robbery might pique your interest," I stated and hoped he took the bait.

The phone was silent for a couple of minutes and then Marcus said, "give me half an hour and I'll be there," and then he hung up. I smiled and said to myself, "game on bitch."

***

I knew that what I was about to tell Brandon was going to break his heart but I had to go get some closure on my situation with Marcus. I lay in the bed and waited for him to come out of the bathroom and when he finally emerged, I got straight to the point.

"I'm going to see Marcus."

He was drying off the beads of water that had attached themselves to his perfectly sculpted body, but my words caused him to cease all motion.

"You're what? Please tell me that I didn't just hear you say that."

I bit my bottom lip because I didn't want to repeat what I'd said but I knew that I had to, "I said I'm going to see Marcus. I have to Brandon. I need to find some closure and I just want to look him in his eyes and ask him why he left me for dead like that. I need to know because I'll never be able to move on until I do."

Brandon sat on the edge of the bed and put his head in the palms of his hands and asked, "Why can't you just live your life and let that shit go?"

"He owes me Brandon, I gave away ten years of my life to protect him and he did me like I didn't mean shit. Like what I'd done for him meant nothing. I have to know why and I want him to pay for it, for every single day I sat behind those gates. God, Brandon, I should have just listened to you but I wanted to believe the best of him," I said while tears filled my eyes.

He pulled me into his embrace and said, "It's over with thought, you're here with me where you belong. Why can't you just let it be?"

I ran a hand down his chest and replied, "Because I'm never going to rest until he feels my pain. You gotta trust me Brandon. I promise you, I'll come back to you."

"Yeah, you said that one time before and I didn't see you for over ten years. Thank God I'm a patient man and believed in what I felt for you but I can't let you do this alone. I'll go with you just in case you need me," He said and kissed my forehead.

"Okay baby, whatever you say," I said and pulled him in for a kiss. He lay back on the bed and I began to kiss down his body until I got to my favorite place.

"Yes baby. Shit, that feels good," he stated in ecstasy when I pulled his manhood into my mouth and brought him to a pleasure he deserved, and then I got on top and rode him until he had nothing left.

When we were done making love, I got out of the bed and went to get us some water. We were out of breath and needed the boost. However, when I put the water in Brandon's glass, I added two pills that would put him to sleep long enough for me to sneak away, "I'm so sorry baby," I said in a whisper. I hated to do things this way but there was no way he was going to let me leave the house without him since I told him of my plans. I didn't need him caught up in any more of my bullshit and I didn't want anything to happen to him. It was something I had to do alone.

I walked back up the stairs and gave him the glass of water and he guzzled it up quickly. "Ah thanks, I damn sure needed that," he said and lay back. I got back in the bed beside him and snuggled up close to him and about five minutes later, I could see his eyelids getting heavy. When they were completely closed, I nudged him and called his name just to make sure he was out, "Brandon, Brandon you asleep already?" When he didn't respond, I knew that I was in the clear. I got up and grabbed the keys to his ride and then went into the safe and took enough money to last me a minute. I left a short note on the table beside the bed and kissed his lips and then walked out.

I hurriedly ran down the stairs and out the front door. I jumped in the ride and looked up toward the window of the room I had just left and said, "Please forgive me baby, I'll be back," and then I drove away.

***

Something in my gut told me that Marcus was lying about being involved in Feelow's muder. I knew that my cousin would do anything to make me feel like shit but when she told me about Marcus killing Feelow, I could see in her eyes that she wasn't intentionally trying to hurt me. I had to get to the bottom of it, especially for Khalif's sake. My son was broken because he had never got the chance to meet his father. The last thing I wanted to do was break him even more by being affiliated with the person who killed his dad.

I had always found it strange that the white girl overpowered Feelow and took his life but I never questioned it because I thought justice had been served and how was it being brought back up? I needed some answers.

When I pulled up to the house, she had just walked out and was about to get in her car. I pulled in behind her so I could block her in. She looked at me and placed her hands on her hips and said angrily, "bitch, get that piece of shit outta my way. I got things to do and don't have time to be fucked up with you."

I turned my car off and got out. I stared her in the eyes until I got right up on her and then said, "I need you to tell me the truth Killisha. For my son's sake, please."

She scrunched up her nose and said, "I have no clue what the hell you are talking about Keisha, you gotta come better than that."

"Oh, you know exactly what I'm talking about bitch. I wanna know if Marcus had anything to do with Feelow's murder, and I'm not leaving here until you tell me something."

"Hmmm, don't tell me you actually listen to anything your crackhead ass cousin tells you. That was probably that shit-talking. Maybe you should go back and question her since she seems to know so damn much," She said with an attitude.

I could tell in her eyes that she knew and I felt like if I pissed her off enough, she'd sing like a bird. "Oh, what's the matter Killisha? You still mad about Marcus pushing all that good dick up in me? Huh? Bitch, it doesn't matter how long you stay with him, he's gonna always crave this pussy, yours will never match up."

I could see that I'd hit her where it hurt and smiled. Her nose flared and I could see her jaw bones flex. She inhaled a long breath of air and said, "Yeah Keisha, any nigga alive is gonna run up in some easy pussy but that's all you'll ever be to hm. I'm the one wearing the ring and living in the nice house and not to mention, the mother of his first born. You could never take my place. He could fuck you every day and you would still not get to enjoy the kind of life he has made for me, so bitch, keep cockin' your legs open while I sit back and collect the rewards."

She reached out and opened her car door and started to get in but I needed to know, so I didn't give up, "Please Killisha, I know you and I have never seen eye to eye but if you know something please tell me. What if the shoe was on the other foot? Wouldn't you want to know?

She ignored me and got in her car and closed the door behind her. I looked at her through pleading eyes and said, "I just need to know if I should walk away and never come back. I can't do this to my son. I can't let his father's murderer be in his life but I don't want to make the wrong decision. Please, just tell me what you can. Please."

Killisha started her car and then rolled down her window and said, "Keisha, I wasn't there the night it happened, so I can't give you details, Marcus is the only one who can do that. Maybe one day when you're sleeping with the enemy, the truth will reveal itself, now I have somewhere I need to be, so could you please move out of my way?"

I pursed my lips together and nodded my head, I could read between the lines of what she'd told me and my heart broke. I held my head down and walked back to my car so I could move out of

Killisha's way. I backed up so she could get by but was too lost in thought to go any further. When she passed by me, I looked up and saw her on her cell phone. I knew in my heart that it was Marcus on the other end of that line. I wondered if she was telling him about our encounter. However, I didn't give a fuck about how he would feel about me questioning her. He took my son's father from him, I just knew it.

"I can't believe that bastard had the nerve to play daddy to my son after he killed his father," I said out loud. I waited a few minutes and then pulled out and began to follow Killisha at a distance. When I thought she'd be off the phone with Marcus, I dialed his number and he answered on the first ring.

"You fucking bastard, all these years yo been in my son's life and you're the reason he doesn't have a father. You piece of shit. I thought he was your best friend Marcus. Why would you kill him?"

"Keisha, calm down and listen to me. I'm not going to do this over the phone. Go home and I'll stop by as soon as I'm done handling this business. There's a lot you don't know. Please, just go home, I'll tell you everything when I get there," He stated in a hurry.

I didn't even respond to him but instead hung up. I threw my phone in the passenger seat and thought about Feelow, "Oh my god, what kind of woman sleeps with her man's murderer? I'm so sorry Feelow. I'm so sorry. Please forgive me."

I looked ahead and remembered that I had Killisha about four cars in front of me and smiled. I saw her turn down a side street and followed. I felt like maybe she knew I had followed her because she sped up, but the bitch wasn't going to get away. She had known all along and never said anything, even though we weren't friends, she could have told me because I would have told her. Not for her sake but for her son's. I owed Marcus for what he had taken from me and he was about to get his karma.

"This is for you Feelow. I got your back," I said out loud and then I sped up.

Chapter Eight

I pulled up to the hotel I had to meet the chic Mya at and got out. I had thought about taking my gun in with me but decided not to. The last thing I needed was a weapons charge. I had no idea what Mya looked like but when I saw the mocha-colored beauty coming toward me, I hoped that it was her.

"Hello Marcus, I'm Mya," she said when she got close to me. I looked her up and down and took in her intoxicating scent. Her beauty alone was lethal and I couldn't wait to get to know her. I was going to play it cool for a minute but I was getting myself some of that.

"Sup Mya, you wanna tell me what you brought me here for?"

She looked at me with a devious smile and replied, "Come on Marcus and follow me. I have us a table away from everyone else."

I walked behind her and watched her ass sway side to side and all I could think about was seeing what was under the jeans she had on. Whoever the btich belonged to was a lucky mutha fucka and never should have let her out of their sight, especially around a nigga like me.

We got to the table and as soon as we sat down, she didn't waste any time. "I'm here because of a woman named Krystal Madison. Are you familiar with her?"

The sound of Krystal's name brought up a lot of memories and made me feel like shit all over again. I felt bad about letting her go to prison for what I'd done but a nigga couldn't afford a murder charge. I know the dumb bitch didn't think I was going to wait for her to come back home. Hell no, I had Killisha and a son to worry about, so I had to push Krystal to the back of my mind.

"Who the fuck is she to you?" I asked with a scowl on my face.

"Hmmm, the bitch ain't nobody to me. I was hoping she meant something to you so you would come and get her so I could have my man back. I worked too fucking hard to keep him to let a bitch come in and pull him from me." She said with attitude but had no idea what the fuck she was talking about. I was getting pissed off at the bitch because I felt like she had wasted my time with the bullshit.

"Look, I know you ain't bring my ass here to play captain save a hoe so if you don't get nothing else for me, I'm outta here," I said and pushed the chair I had sat in back from the table, when I stood she stood with me and grabbed my wrist.

"Please, just listen. I'm not done."

The look in her eyes made me submit and I sat back down and said, "If you don't give me something to keep my interest within the next five minutes, my ass is outta here."

"Okay, alright," she said and looked around the room before she locked eyes with me. My dick stood at attention while I watched her lips move and imagined them around the head of my manhood, "Krystal showed up at B-Lines a little over a week ago and that mutha fucka dissed me. I've put in eight long fucking years with him and this bitch just comes in and pulls him from me, like it wasn't shit."

Before she had a chance to say anything else I cut her off, "Wait a fucking minute, Krystal is with B-Line? That explains it. That explains why that mutha fucka cut me off. I knew it."

"Wait, I'm not done. I and him had fallen out one night because the bastard called me by her name while I was giving him head but his ass tried to convince me that I was imagining shit. I got angry and left him with a soft dick but felt bad and went back to try and make amends. However, when I got to the condo, that bitch whose name he called me by was there. That hoe answered his door and everything, something I wasn't ever allowed to do. Anyway, he dissed me right in front of her and his fucking friends and made me feel like shit. I stormed out but instead of leaving, I stood in the foyer and listened to what they were talking about and that's when I saw her ID card from prison on the table. I wanted to learn more about her so I could hopefully make him turn against her so I took a photo of the card on my phone and when I googled her, an article about a murder came up and that's how I got our name."

One thing I could admit, the bitch was long-winded and when she finally stopped talking, I asked, "What the hell does all that have to do with what you told me on the phone? I could give a fuck about that bitch but I need to know about the robbery you were talking about."

She pursed her lips together and raised her eyebrows and told me what I wanted to know, "That's what they were talking about when I was eavesdropping in the foyer. They said something about jacking someone for some bricks while they were at a club. I'm not sure who they were talking about but it could be useful information for you to use."

"That mutha fucker," I said and couldn't believe that the information about the robbery of my drugs, fell right into my lap. I was going to dick the bitch in front of me down real good as a reward for what she'd given me. I pulled my phone out of my pocket and began to dial but she stopped me.

"Wait, who are you calling?" She asked.

"I'm calling my boy. Those drugs belonged to me and someone is going to pay for them," I stated anxiously. I couldn't believe that Krystal had gotten out of prison and run to B-Line. I had felt all along that he'd had a thing for her but brushed it off and now I wish I would have believed in my instincts.

"Look, I don't give a fuck about the bitch but Brandon is off limits. You have to promise me that," she pleaded through desperate eyes. I hung up without talking to anyone, but she had the game fucked up if she thought that I'd let B-line slide for helping Krystal rob me. Krystal had to have gotten her information from someone and I knew it had to be him. However, I'd let Mya think that B-line was in the clear because I'm sure she would let him know what she told me. I could see why it was so easy for B-line to let the bitch walk away. She was beyond beautiful and probably had some good pussy but her ass didn't know shit about the game. If she did, then she never would have come to me. I wasn't a dumb ass nigga and I knew that if she was disloyal to a man she'd been fucking for years, her ass had the potential to be disloyal to me. I would use her ass until I could get what I wanted and then I would make her ass vulture food.

I looked her straight in the eyes and lied, "aight, I give you my word. I won't touch B-line but I'm going to make Krystal pay for every single brick and when I'm done, she'll be out of your way and you can live happily ever after with your prince," no sooner than I got the words out, my cell phone rang and when I saw it was my wife's number, I answered. "What's good?" I didn't want Mya to know that I had a wife because I felt like I could get more out of her if she thought I was single, so I didn't show any emotions when I answered the phone. However, the news that came from the other end made my heart skip a beat," I'm on my way."

***

On my way back to town, I made a pit stop and hoped that I was successful with who I came to see. When I pulled up to the warehouse, it looked abandoned and it made me wonder if he was still there. I got out of the car and proceeded to walk up the short concrete path that led to the door, but before I had a chance to knock, it opened up.

"Well, well, well. I feel like I'm in some kind of dream. Heard about your little trip, glad to see you made it out, okay, but what brings you to my neck of the woods?"

"Hello Temple, it's good to know that you haven't forgotten me," I said with a smile.

"How could I forget something so beautiful? Please, come in and let's talk."

He opened the door wider so I could walk inside and everything seemed to appear as it did before. One would never know that the walls were filled with high-tech machinery and ammo because of the way it was set up. However, I knew of the power my surroundings held because that's what I was there for.

"I'm here on business, Temple but I need it to stay between us."

"Ah, you want to make sure that Marcus doesn't learn of your visit, am I correct?"

"Well, yeah. He doesn't know that I'm back and I'd like to keep it that way."

Temple went to his small bar and poured himself a drink. After he emptied the glass, he pulled a small lever that even I hadn't noticed and the walls opened.

"The business I do with you is of no one else's concern. Your secret will be safe with me."

"Thank you Temple."

I walked over to the open wall and browsed until I saw the perfect one. "I want that one," I said and pointed to a gold-plated nine-millimeter; I wanted Marcus to know that I meant business when I saw him and the gun was very intimidating.

Temple lifted an eyebrow and said, "Ah, a lady with expensive taste. That's a nice choice and it would look even lovelier in your hands. Are you shooting to kill or just to stun?"

"Uh uh. A girl never tells, so you'll just have to continue to wonder."

Temple pulled the gun from the rack that it hung on and turned to ask me, "And how many clips are you going to need with this?"

I thought about his question and replied, "I think one will do just fine."

He pulled down the clip and an extra box of ammo and passed it to me. The gun felt foreign in my small hands and reminded me of the times when I meant something to Marcus, or at least when I thought I meant something. I put the gun and ammo in my bag and asked Temple, "What do I owe you?"

He shook his head and said, "nothing. I think you've paid enough by showing your loyalty to a mother fucker who didn't deserve you. What I just handed you is what you have already earned. Just promise me, you won't miss."

I remained quiet because I really didn't know what to say. Temple was right though, I had already paid enough and now it would be Marcus' time to pay me back.

"I won't miss and even though he taught me everything I know, he won't see me coming."

"Shall I send a couple of my men with you?"

"No Temple, this is something that I got to do myself. Enough people have suffered just from what happened. The only one who didn't is about to feel my pain."

***

"So, does Marcus know that I'm still alive?" She asked when she came out of the bathroom.

I stared at her form and replied, "What do you think? That's why you gotta stay put, at least for now."

"Did you tell him that you already killed me and get your money?"

"You are asking a lot of questions for a btich who has a bounty over her head. Questions you already know the answer to. Your ass got on a wire or something?" I asked and gave her a crazy look.

She dropped the towel she'd had around her and replied, "You're more than welcome to search me if you'd like."

As soon as I saw her naked form, my dick rocked up but I wasn't the only one who noticed. Tammy said seductively, "looks like your flashlight is ready to search the cave."

It had been a minute since I'd been up in something warm so I said, "Why don't you come on over here and flip the switch on this mutha fucka."

As soon as I said it, she was on me. Tammy pulled out my dick and gave me that slow head. I could feel my toes curl from the pressure. "Shit," was all I could get out. Tammy's head game was on point but the last thing I wanted to do was waste a nut in it, so I pushed her head up and said, "Come on and lay that ass down so I can give you a reason to stay put."

Tammy did as I said and lay back on the bed. I put her legs on my shoulders so I could go deep in the pussy. Although she had been on the block for a minute, her pussy was still nice and tight. "Oh my God Terrance, I haven't been fucked like this in a while, shit, it feels so good."

"You like this dick Tammy? Huh?"

"Yes Terrance, yes. I love this dick."

I sped up and pounded into her harder as I watched her ample breasts bounce up and down. My nut sack slapped her ass every time I pushed my dick inside of her.

"Tell me how much you love it Tammy. Tell me how good this mutha fucka is to you," I said in the heat of passion.

"It's so damn good. Fuck me Terrance. Please don't stop. Please."

I felt the sweat form on my forehead as my nuts swelled and prepared to release the unfertilized seeds they had held for so long, "Damn, this pussy is good," I cried out and pushed in hard one last time and released all my babies into her. The shit was so good, I couldn't have pulled out if I wanted to.

Afterwards, we took a shower together and were about to go for round two when a knock suddenly came on the door. As far as I knew, no one knew about the place I had put Tammy up in, so I drew my weapon and put a finger over my lips to tell Tammy to be quiet. I got to the door and looked out the peephole and saw Trap standing outside the door.

"Open the door Tag. I'm by myself," he said from outside.

I turned around and grabbed some pants and told Tammy to get dressed and go in the bathroom and then I opened the door. "Ain't no sense in hiding her dawg, I know you weren't going to kill her," Trap said as he walked inside the apartment.

I shut the door behind him and asked, "Who all knows?"

"Man, shit just doesn't look right with you suddenly being out of the loop. You can keep her alive but you gotta stay in a routine. You have been a ghost ever since Marcus gave you the job."

Tammy walked out of the bathroom and asked in a fearful voice, "Are you going to tell Marcus that I'm still alive?"

Trap looked her up and down because Tammy cleaned up nicely and since she'd been with me, she had smoked none of that crack shit, so she was also getting her weight back up. "Ya know, Marcus is my nigga and all but I ain't no snitch. You ain't a threat to me and as long as you stay put and listen to Tag, you won't be a threat to him either. But I didn't come here for that. I got other shit you need to know about Tag."

"Have a seat man, what's going on out there?"

"You need to get your ass back on the scene, ya girl Swag made that Brooklyn trip for the forty and was jacked on the way back."

"What? Man, I'm a kill me a bitch about my people," I stated angrily, I couldn't believe that someone had the nerve to try the crew like that.

"Don't worry Tag, she aight. Apparently, she likes to frequent some strip clubs on the way back from pickups. While she was inside getting entertained, someone took the forty out of the compartment."

I thought for a minute and then said, "so whoever jacked her had to have known where the stash was in the car. She never takes the same vehicle, so this had to be an inside job."

"Don't worry, Marcus is on it. He got a call from some chick named Mya saying she knew who jacked the goods."

"What? Tell me man. What the fuck are you waiting on? Who the fuck robbed my mutha fuckin people?"

Trap looked at me with a crazy glint in his eyes and said, "Krystal."

***

I pulled into the hospital and parked my car at the front entrance. A parking ticket was the least of my worries.

When someone from the hospital called me from Killi's phone and told me she'd been in an accident, my mind went into murder mode. Killi was the safest driver I knew and although things happen, something told me that it was intentional.

I ran straight to the front desk and stated, "Excuse me, my wife Killisha Newsome was in an accident. They called me from here, could you please tell me where I can find her." The nurse looked at me with beady eyes through small metal-framed glasses and then punched some keys on the keyboard. A minute later, she gave me the information I'd asked for, "yes, your wife was brought here about two hours ago and she is in room 317."

I ran to the elevator and pushed the number three and although I had never prayed before, I did my best, "Dear god, please let her be alright. I know I've done some shit that I shouldn't have but please spare her. Take me instead if you have to." I closed my eyes and pinched the bridge of my nose and when the elevator door dinged, I rushed out. I knew that I had not always been the greatest man to Killisha but I truly loved her. She had been through it all with me and never once turned her back. I told myself that if God spared her, I would change my ways and do right by her, from that day on.

I found room 317 and pushed the door open. What I saw almost took my breath away. She was hooked to all kinds of machines and what looked like a breathing tube. I could feel the tears form in my eyes and instead of holding them in, I let them go. I knew that it had all been my fault. It was my karma for all the things I'd done to others who didn't deserve it and I couldn't be mad at anybody but myself.

"Excuse me, sir. I need to ask you to leave, visiting hours are over."

The voice had brought me out of my stupor and I raised my head to look at Killi one more time. "Don't worry baby. I'm going to make her pay for this," I said and squeezed her hand. I kissed her on the forehead and then walked out. I got in my car and remembered that I had never even asked the nurse what Killi's chances were. I guessed that maybe I hoped that God would answer my prayer.

I drove out of the parking lot and went straight to Keisha's. I didn't know what led me there but I had to go somewhere familiar. When she opened the door, she could sense right away that something was wrong. "Oh my God Marcus, are you okay? Did something happen to Markill?" I walked inside without answering her and she closed the door behind me. I pulled her into a tight hug because I knew it would be the last time she'd allow it. I had decided to confess what I'd done to Feelow because one of us needed peace of mind. I figured it would keep any more karma from coming my way.

"Killi was in an accident and she ain't doing too good."

"Damn Marcus, I'm so sorry, I mean, I can't stand that bitch but if there's anything I can do just say the word and I got you."

"Keisha, we need to talk about something and I just need you to hear me out, okay."

"Yeah, okay Marcus, let's go sit down in the living room. Khalif's in his room playing so we'll have some privacy."

I followed Keisha to the living room and sat down beside her on the couch. I knew that no matter what she said, our relationship was about to change forever. I told myself that I should at least get the pussy one more time but thought better of it. I had done some foul shit but to fuck Killish's enemy while she lied in a hospital and fought for her life would be the ultimate betrayal and I had vowed to change if God spared her.

"Marcus, could you just say what you need to say?" Keisha exclaimed.

I looked into her eyes and began, "I lied to you about Feelow."

She scrunched her eyebrows and stood up from the couch and asked, "What? What the hell do you mean, lied? Quit beating around the fucking bush Marcus and just spit that shit out."

"I killed Feelow Keisha. I'm sorry but he gave me no other choice. You know that he was after me and I had to make the decision to get to him before he got to me."

Keisha remained calm and stated. "So you let the white girl take the fall for it so you wouldn't have to go to prison."

"Yes, I made her feel guilty and she ultimately did what she had to do to save me but instead of sticking by her while she was there, I left her to fend for herself and she's out wreaking havoc on my life."

"Why did you do it Marcus? Yall could have made up like you always did. That was your brother. That was my son's father, you bastard. You took him from Khalif before he even had a chance to meet him. Don't you have any kind of heart?"

"Keisha, I need you to understand that it was something I had to do. I brought him into this thing and he was slowly knocking down my men. He had a nigga named Trigger take out Blow and Black, two of my top men. He was trying to go against me, even to the point of taking my life. He had gotten out of hand and lost control for God's sake Keisha, he was going to kill your ass too."

"Yeah, Marcus, but he didn't. Once he would have laid eyes on Khalif it would have changed his heart. He would have loved me even more once he saw what we had created together. He was hurt, Marcus. He thought you had set him up to test his loyalty and then you had the fucking nerve to put a white bitch in his spot beside you. How did you think he was going to feel?"

Keisha was right, maybe I did create the monster that Feelow had become but he never should have questioned my loyalty. "Yeah, Keisha, I did put her over shit that he had been running but he was fucking up my business. He started pulling bread out of the oven and accusing niggas that had never done me wrong of taking it. He would have only gotten worse and that shit had his ass paranoid as fuck. Keisha, he wouldn't have spared you no matter how many sons you would have given him."

"Marcus, please leave and don't ever come back here. I don't want you in Khalif's life either. What kind of mother would I be to allow his father's murderer through my front door?"

"Come on Keisha, don't do this. You have to find it in your heart to forgive me, at least for Khalif's sake, I'm the closest thing to a father he has ever had." I pleaded but my words fell on deaf ears.

Keisha walked out the front door and opened it and then said, "No Marcus, you took away the closest thing Khalif had for a father. Now get the hell out of our lives."

I walked to the door and stood in front of her. I knew that I would come to Keisha never speaking to me again but I had to get rid of the burden I had carried for so long. Maybe, God would spare Killi in exchange for what I had confessed.

"I'm a leave but just know that if you ever need me, I'm there. Tell my nephew I love him and I'm sorry," I said and then walked out of Keisha and Khalif's life forever. It was time for me to find Krystal and I knew just where to go to locate her.

***

I had already known that Marcus killed Feelow because although I and Tammy weren't close anymore, I knew she would have never made up something like that. I wondered if Marcus had done something to Tammy too because it wasn't like her to just vanish from thin air.

I smiled at the thought of Killisha lying in that hospital as she fought for her life and it brought me even more pleasure to know that Marcus thought the white girl had something to do with it. After I pulled out and followed Killisha for a few miles, visions of Feelow lying in that casket came to my mind. Eleven years later, he was still the love of my life and although I continued to fuck with Marcus over the years, Feelow remained with me.

When I saw Kilisha turn down a side street, I knew that she had finally spotted me behind her, but instead of speeding up to get away from me, the dumb bitch slowed down and was about to pull over. I then went around her vehicle and drove up the road away before I turned back around. I wanted the bitch to look me in my eyes when I rammed into her. I made sure my seatbelt was secure and put my foot on the gas. I could see her car come into view and it gave me the momentum to push the gas harder.

"This is for you Feelow," I said out loud and went through with my plan.

Protege of a Legend 3

The impact was hard and when my airbag deployed, I felt supreme satisfaction. I hoped that I had killed the bitch but knew that I couldn't stick around to find out. I hoped that my car wasn't so badly wrecked that I couldn't get out of there. I breathed a sigh of relief when I was able to back up and drive away.

My body had already begun to feel the effects of the crash even before I got too far away. I drove straight to the chop shop that an older trick of mine owned. I knew that all I had to do was ride the dick real good and he would cover up everything.

"Damn Keisha, the fuck did you hit?" Monsta asked as soon as I pulled into his garage.

"It doesn't matter what I hit, just get rid of the car for me. I also need you to give me another one and Monsta, you know this has to stay between us."

"Yeah, yeah, yeah. I got you but what's in it for me?"

I had already known what he would require from me and although my chest and arms were bruised up from the impact, I stripped off all my clothes and fucked him like he had the last dick on earth.

"Damn girl, that pussy can make a mutha fucker forget his name, shit," He said when we had finished fucking.

He pulled his coveralls back on and handed me a set of keys to a car that was identical to mine. No one would have been the wiser.

"Thanks Monsta." I said and grabbed the keys from him.

"No problem. Feel free to crash anytime you like," He stated with a smile.

I got in the car and drove away from the evidence of my sin. Once I got back on the highway and headed home, I said to myself, "an eye for an eye mother fucker."

Corey Robinson

Chapter Nine

"Mya, what's good?" I asked as soon as she picked up the phone. I felt that it was time I paid her another visit.

"Oh, hey Marcus. I'm glad to hear from you again. What can I help you with?" She asked.

"Aye, a nigga feeling a little lonely. I was hoping I could stop by. Maybe we could make plans to make some things happen for both of us. You feel like a little company."

"Um yeah, you know I was about to go out and do some shopping but I think I can put that off until later. Come on by."

"Bet, I'll be there in a few," I hung up and sat in my ride for a minute. I was in the parking lot of the hotel she stayed in but didn't want her to know that I was so close. That bitch was going to give me all the answers I needed to find Krystal. Although Mya had said that she was with B-line, something told me that she was closer than that. I knew that it was her that had caused Killi's accident as if robbing Swag for my dope wasn't enough. I wondered what else she had up her sleeve and needed to locate her before anything else happened. I screwed the silence on to the end of my gun and pulled my hoodie over my head. The shades that covered my face would hide enough. I had parked around the back of the hotel and planned on getting rid of it when I was done.

I finally got out and took the stairs to the third floor instead of the elevator. I knew that other people would be less likely to be on the stairs. When I got to her floor, I stuck my head out and made sure no one was around and then I knocked on Mya's door.

She opened it like she was in a rush and when I walked in, I noticed the bra and thong set that she had on. The thongs set between her ass cheeks perfectly and left nothing to the imagination. I could see her nipples as they poked out from the white lace of the bra and licked my lips.

She smiled and stated, "Um, I could put something on if this makes you uncomfortable."

I licked my lips and replied, "Nah, as a matter of fact, you can take that shit off."

My dick rocked up and I swore that it would bust through the zipper on my Sean John jeans. Mya seductively removed what little she wore and then lied back on the bed and spread her mocha-colored legs. Her pussy opened right up as if to welcome me to its center. I wondered just how many licks it would take to make her bust a nut in my mouth, a bitch that fine had to taste like strawberries.

I knew that no matter what, I had to stick to my plan. I would fuck the bitch on the bed good and proper and then get her to tell me as much as she could and then I would send her to her creator. "Damn, what a waste," I said so low, there was no way she could have heard me.

"What's the matter Marcus? You act like you're scared of a little pussy," she said while she put her hand between her legs and played with her clit. I watched from the sideline and said nothing. I wanted the btich to make herself cum and then I would take over from there. "Oh yes. Come on Marcus you gonna make me do this all by myself?"

I finally came out of my clothes, careful not to let the gun be seen and then I pulled a condom out of my pants pocket. I couldn't afford to have my DNA found in the bitch.

"Come on Mya. Show a nigga how to make that pussy cum."

I couldn't believe that B-line had let such a gem go but then I thought about how she ran to me and told me about the jack. B-line was a smart nigga and had probably already known she was disloyal. That's why he dissed her as soon as the most loyal bitch I knew showed up at his front door.

"Oh shit, Marcus. Come on and let me have some of that dick. Nigga, I know that big bitch has got some power behind it." Her talking shit made me harder and I continued to watch her until I saw the creamy essence at her entrance. That's when I went in for the kill, I pushed a finger inside of her and pulled it out. I put it in my mouth so I could test the product. "It tastes good to you Marcus? Huh? This pussy could cum all night if you make it. There's plenty more where that came from."

"Yeah, but I bet you ain't neva had a nigga fuck you like I'm about to. B-line's fuck game ain't got shit on me. You better brace yourself." I said and got between her thighs. I put my dick at her entrance and pushed in as hard and fast as I could. I almost pulled out and took the condom off because her shit was tight and plenty wet. I wanted to feel the real deal but knew that I couldn't afford to.

"Damn, this pussy good as fuck, throw that shit back, wet this dick all up."

She jacked her clit and thrust up while I pushed into her. "Yes, yes nigga I'm about to fucking squirt all over this mutha fucka, shit. Fuck me Marcus. Oh my God, this is some good dick."

I was proud that I could make her last fuck worth it. I sped up a little faster and not even thirty seconds later, I filled the condom with children that would never be born. I slowed my pace and when I pulled out, the condom was covered in her sticky wetness. I pulled it off and took it to the restroom where I flushed it and then went back to the bed and sat on the edge of it beside Mya.

"Shit girl, that was good, you surprised me," I exclaimed.

"Yeah Marcus, I agree. It was amazing. Shit, you could make a girl like me forget all about Brandon or anyone else for that matter."

"Speaking of B-line, I had some people go up there to see him but he was ghost. I was good business to him and I was just trying to understand his move. Any idea where he could be?"

"No, actually. I only know about the condo. He had never told me much about his business and he never allowed me to go with him to Jambo and Carrie's. I guess he just wanted to keep me safe.

I didn't say shit when she mentioned the name Carrie. I had always wondered what that crazy bitch had gotten off to and never guessed she went to Baltimore. I know that B-line probably kept Mya out of his business because he knew she was a snake, and would one day show her disloyalty. "So his partner and his partner's girl were in on the jack too."

"I heard them say something about Carrie and a dance but I don't know for sure that it had anything to do with the jack. They could have been talking about another club."

I looked at her to see if I could catch a lie and asked, "Any idea what they were going to do with the drugs they took?"

"No, once I took a picture of the girl's ID, my ass was out of there."

"Hmmm. So you been fucking that nigga for years but yet, it's that easy for you to come to me, someone you don't even know and sell him out. You don't feel bad about that shit?"

"Hell no. Why should I? His ass asked for it when he dissed me for that white bitch. I owed him that."

"Yeah, that's kinda what I thought you would say. So, I guess you fucked me as part of your payback too, huh?"

"Well, the dick I guess was a little bonus for me. It was a nice reward and I hope that you're gonna lay that pipe to me again without information. I'd make that trip from Baltimore every day for that good dick."

"Nah, I don't think you gonna ever be making this trip again. I don't have room in my camp for a disloyal bitch. The last person that stabbed me in the back, found themself in the dirt. I think I'll be better without you," I stated and stood up from the bed. I picked up my clothes and got dressed while she sat there with a confused look on her face.

"I would never be disloyal to you Marcus, I could actually be a great asset to you."

"Nah Mya I'm good. You turned on a mutha fucka that you been fuckin for years just because he got another bitch up in the crib. What the fuck kind of loyalty is that? Bitch, if you'll turn on him that easy, then that shows me that you'll turn on me too. Instead of hating on Krystal though, you should have asked for her advice on how to maintain beside a street nigga because that mouth of yours is putting you six feet deep."

I pulled out my gun and before Mya had a chance to scream, I put a bullet between her eyes. I left the bitch lying on the bed with eyes wide open. She deserved more than that, though. I had no respect for snakes even when they called themselves looking out for me. If you are disloyal to my enemy, then you'll be disloyal to me too. I had to silence her before anyone found out she had ever been affiliated with me, even if I had only been for a brief minute.

I pulled the small bottle of bleach I'd gotten out of my travel kit out of my pocket and wiped down anything that I may have touched. I even wiped down Mya's body with it. I then carefully walked back out of the room and retraced my steps back to my ride. The parking lot was dark but not so dark I didn't notice the flat tires.

"What the fuck," I stated angrily, "That bitch."

I knew in my heart that Krystal had flattened all my tires. I could feel her presence and looked around the parking lot.

"I know you're here. Come on out so we can handle this shit like two adults. What the fuck you came back here for anyway? I should be the last person you'd want to see."

About that time, a figure emerged from the bushes. I drew my gun but when I realized that four red beams were on my chest, I lowered it.

"Hello Marcus. Did you miss me? Of course you did. Oh, thanks for taking care of Mya for me. It makes my life much easier to know you had my back, but you should have had it way before now."

I could only see the outline of her body and her face because she had on all black. Her voice made my stomach bubble with nervousness. I had taught her very well, so I knew what she was capable of, so I tried to reason with her.

"Come on Krys. That shit is in the past. Let's move past it. You got your payback when you ran into my wife. Let's squash this shit." I hollered out.

"Your wife. That wasn't me Marcus. You can thank your other piece of pussy for that one, Keisha beat me to it"

"What? Keisha?"

"Yeah. I thought you knew. It's you I wanted, not your bitch. Marcus, you left me for dead after I gave up everything for you. Even if you would have just acknowledged what I'd done for you, we might have been okay but your black ass forgot all about me and now I'm back to make your life a living hell. Make sure you watch your back at all times. Oh yeah, and thanks for the come-up."

I stood there and waited for her to say something else but only silence came. I looked down and saw that the red beams were gone from my chest and took off toward the way she'd come but she was long gone. I had never been scared of a mutha fucka but Krystal was a scorned woman and their fury outweighed anything I could have imagined.

***

"I heard you have something that belongs to me," Tetris said through the phone as soon as I answered it.

I thought about what he'd said and responded in code, "Nah playa, I'd say you and my pops should be even now."

Tetris had been my father's competition back in the day and had one of his street crews run up in one of his stash houses. He came off with fifty bricks and instead of my father waging a war, he told Tetris, "You can keep those but remember, you will always be in my debt. I don't want a war with you. The streets have been quiet. Let's keep it that way."

It took Tetris a minute to respond to what I'd said but when he did, I was pleased with his answer, "you're a good kid and your father would be proud of you. We're even, have a good life, and enjoy the fruits of your labor." He then hung up and left me on the line with a clear conscience about what had gone down. I'd never had a street war because my father had been the smartest player on the board. He grounded me from a young age and taught me how to keep peace among men.

I had expected the call from Tetris but hoped that it was Krystal. She hadn't contacted me since she'd been gone. I couldn't believe that she'd drugged me so she could slip away. I had almost followed her when I woke up but my pops always said, "when a woman leaves, let her go. If she says she'll be back, you gotta trust that she will but never go after her. Although my pops was no longer around, I took all he had taught me to heart and would never forget it.

Carrie had asked me if I wanted her to go and bring Krystal back but my response was, "Nah, if she comes back before she does what she needs to do, she'll never be satisfied and she'll never be able to devote herself completely to me. She'll be back on her own and all I can do is wait for her."

Carrie said with a smile, "Well, if you need me to go beat someone's ass, just say the word," and I knew that she was serious.

I'd heard through my sources that Mya had shown up to find Marcus. My guess was she had overheard our conversation about the robbery and went to inform Marcus although he was a stranger to her. If I knew Marcus like I thought I did, then Mya was dead by now, and he would be more concerned with Krystal than me, however, I stayed ready just in case.

***

"Oh, so you were able to come outta that cracked-out pussy long enough to check on us," Swag said with an attitude. If she would have been a man, I would have punched the shit out of her.

"Bitch, if your ass wouldn't have been getting entertained by strange pussy, you wouldn't be in the position you're in now. Who the fuck do you think you talking to?" I exclaimed.

Echo walked in and tried to make peace, "hey, hey, hey. Y'all talking shit to each other ain't gonna change nothing. Both you mutha fuckas are wrong, so shut the fuck up and let's figure this shit out."

"The fuck is there to figure out? Swag's stupid ass knows she ain't pose to make pit stops when she's out on a run. What the fuck was she trunking?" I asked while I looked at Swag crazy.

Echo said, "Ain't nothing we can do to change what happened but we gotta come together and make up a plan to get the money

Corey Robinson

to pay Tetris ass for those forty we lost. We owe him six hundred thousand dollars, so let's put our bread up and make the shit right and then we'll go from there."

"Hell no, that shit ain't my responsibility. That shit is on Swag, so take me out of the equation. I work too fucking hard and take too many chances for me to have to take from myself to pay on some shit I ain't got nothing to do with," I said to Echo. I had only touched the dope a few times over the years. It just wasn't my thing. I made my money by the gun and risked my life every time I went out on a kill.

"Come on Tag, we a fucking team no matter what part we play on the field. We suppose to have each other's backs. What the fucks is wrong with you man? Tammy got you wide open already. You better man the fuck up and act right. This shit falls on all of us like always."

I know that Echo was right. We had always looked out for each other even when the other was in the wrong. That was why our crew had never been touched and if we divided, it would weaken our pact.

"Aight man, my bad but that butch ass bitch betta not come at me sideways again regardless of where I stick my dick at." I said and looked at Swag with a unit on my face."

"Nigga fuck you and that crackhead ass bitch. That hoe 'pose to be six feet deep by now. I'm outta here yo," Swag said and started to walk out but I grabbed her by the arm and pulled her to me to stop her.

"Come on sis. What the fuck are we doing?" I asked.

She smiled and then we gave each other some dap and then Echo said, "Now that's more like it."

We all sat around the table and came up with our plan to pay Tetris his money. I have divided it three ways, we'd be outta the heat.

Swag asked, "What about Marcus? Nigga knows he's a pussy baby. He gon' want some type of compensation."

"Where the fuck he is? That nigga was getting that shit on consignment so his ass is out of fucking gas," Echo said with authority.

"Aye, Tag, how the hell you found out what happened? You way cross the line with your new project so how did you hear?" Swag asked me.

I answered him with a serious tone, "Dawg, Trap came and told me. Somehow he knew where to find me and he knew that Tammy was still alive but I never asked him where he got his information from."

Swag asked, "If Trap knows, then you think that Marcus knows too?"

My heart sped up from the thought of what she'd asked me, "I gotta go," I jumped up from the table and ran back out to my car so that I could go and check on Tammy. I had never known Trap to be a flawed nigga but I also knew that I couldn't put anything past anyone. If Tammy had been touched, I would make it my business to push Trap's wig back.

***

I couldn't believe what I'd heard when he came over, he actually confessed to killing my daddy. I knew that when he left, my momma would want to tell me the news but she would have to wait until I returned.

While she was at the front door telling him he had to leave, I snuck out the sliding glass doors and climbed down using the fire escape ladder. There was no way I'd let him get away with what he'd done.

It was dark but out and getting late, so I decided to stay in the shadows just in case my momma came out to look for me. All my life, I had looked up to the man who killed my daddy and the thought of it made me sick to my stomach. I was ready to off the white girl but she had ended up being a victim too.

I passed a couple of crackheads in an alley and thought of my daddy. I couldn't believe that he used to do what they were doing. My momma had no clue that I knew about his habit but still, he was the greatest and because of my uncle Marcus, I'd never get to know him.

"Hey, hey, lil Feelow, you got a little something I can hold?"

I looked up when I heard the voice and saw old man Sam with his hand held out. He used to cop dope from my daddy but those days had long gone by.

"Nah Sammie, you know I don't sell that shit. I'm too young." I said to him.

"You ain't never too young to make that paper lil Fee. Shit, you should be out here representing your pops."

Little did Sam know, I already was. I had about seventeen dollars in my pocket and pulled it out. I put two dollars back in it and handed the rest to him and said "Here's a few dollars Sam. You should be able to get yourself a little something with it."

He smiled at me and said, "Thanks lil Fee. your pops would be proud," and then he ran off in the opposite direction so he could go get himself a fix.

I was about a block from my destination and the closer I got, the harder my heart beat. I rounded the corner and the bright lights seemed to light up the entire area around it. I looked both ways and crossed the street.

When I walked in, everyone seemed to be in their own zone and didn't notice me at all. I wasn't sure where to go, so I went to the desk where an older white lady had sat only seconds before. I was a smart kid and knew how to use a computer. So when I typed in the name, it gave me the information I needed. No sooner than I walked away, the older lady appeared back behind the counter.

I hopped on the elevator with the rest of the crowd and got off on the fourth floor. I found the room I was looking for and pushed the door open. There she lay with tubes and machines hooked to her. I had never seen her so helpless and wondered if she was in pain.

I closed the door and locked it behind me and then walked up closer to her bedside. I reached my hand out and touched hers and hoped that one day she and God would forgive me for what I was about to do. I ran my fingers down the tube that stuck out of her mouth and then looked over at the machine that beeped.

I breathed in heavily and then exhaled and said "I'm sorry auntie Killi but someone has to pay." I then looked up toward the ceiling and said, "this is for you daddy. Now you can rest in peace."

Chapter Ten

"Thanks fellas, good looking out," I said to King and Killa.

Killa walked up to me and said, "Didn't I tell your pale white ass that you would always have my loyalty?"

I smiled and replied, "yeah, you did tell me that and you kept your word."

I had met King and Killa years ago when Marucs first put me in charge of the deliveries and pickups. King warmed to me immediately but Killa tried my patience. He refused to take orders from a white girl and played tough but when I showed him that I could hold my own and I was not to be fucked with, he got with the program. He had promised me that no matter what, he would always have my back and all these years later, his word was still his bond.

"I don't understand why you ain't let us blast his ass," King stated and I could hear the disappointment in his voice.

"Shit, that mutha fucka deserves whatever's coming his way for that fuck shit he let you go through. I thought Marcus' ass was thorough but he is a fucking pussy and I don't respect that shit at all," Killa said and then pulled on the blunt he held between his fingers.

"It's all good boys. This is my beef, so I want to handle it my way. If anyone takes Marcus out, it will be me but honestly, I don't want to kill him, I just want to make him wish he was dead."

"Well, anytime you're ready to light his ass up, just give us a call," King exclaimed.

I wondered why it was so easy for them to follow me when they had worked under Marcus for so long. I decided that the only way to find out was to ask, "Hey, what happened to make yall turn away from Marcus? I thought yall were cool with him."

Killa answered me, "Yeah, we were cool with him at one time but that mutha fucka got beside himself and thought that we could just start chump changing us, a nigga had bills and shit to pay but was barely making ends meet. Then I fucked around and got my girl pregnant and the money he was paying wasn't enough to feed my seed, so I told him to kiss my ass and got a new connect, and as you can see, I'm doing much better."

King cut in and stated, "We can actually sit back and chill a little now without worrying about the shit we need. Plus, that foul ass shit he did to you put the icing on the cake. You should let fuck boy take his own change. I'm sure the block would have been just fine without his black ass."

"It's all good. Doing that time just made me stronger and even more motivated. I'm going to get him right where I want him and then I'm going to take all my frustration out on him and trust me, I got a lot of that built up."

We shared a laugh and passed around the blunt that Killa had lit and reminisced on the old times. I stayed a little longer than I'd anticipated and when I noticed the time, I said, "Hey boys, it's been great but a bitch has things to do, so I'm going to be on my way."

"Aight, but don't forget us when you go in and infiltrate his ass."

"Yeah, at least, let us come watch."

"I got yall, so don't worry," I gave both of them a hug and walked out.

I was driving to the hotel where I had been staying and another thought came to my mind. I turned on the next exit and went where my heart told me to go. I was nervous as hell when I knocked on the door and hoped that the person who lived there didn't turn me away. I waited a few minutes but when no one came to the door, I turned around and walked away and as soon as I put my foot down on the first step, I heard a voice come from behind me, "Can I help you with something?"

I turned around and walked back to the door and stared Keisha in the eyes. "Hi Keisha, I'm ...

"I know who you are but what I'm trying to figure out is why you are at my door."

"Look, I just want to talk to you, please." She continued to stare at me but said nothing. I could read the pain in her eyes and wondered if she could also read mine. I thought about my next move but figured it would be the only way she would let me in. I pushed up the sleeves of my jacket and turned my arms over. I could feel tears well up in my eyes and did nothing to stop them.

I finally spoke again, "I did this to myself while I was in prison. I just wanted to die so the pain in my heart would go away but they saved me and I lived another day. A week before I was to leave, I did this one, "I pointed to the downward slit that had left an ugly scar and continued, "I didn't want to come out of there because I thought that I was broken beyond repair but I was saved again. I couldn't understand why God kept sparing me but I stopped questioning it and here I am. If God could forgive me, then I feel like I have a purpose, so could you please just let me in and hear me out?"

Keisha looked like I'd touched something in her, I just hoped I'd pierced her heart enough to hear me out. She stood and stared at me for a couple of more minutes and then slowly opened the door far enough for me to enter, and said, "You got one shot, so this better be good."

We walked into her living room and sat down opposite each other. I had planned on starting the conversation but she beat me to it, "I know the truth and I'm just curious why you would give up your life like that for someone like Marcus."

I smiled when I heard his name because, at one time in my life, he meant the world to me. I didn't want to leave anything out so I started from the beginning, "I lost my parents before I became an adult and once they were gone, I had no one and nowhere to go. I had started living from alley to alley and one day I was grabbed in the same alleys I'd found peace in. I was grabbed by Feelow and Marcus saved me, or better yet, acted like he had."

She cut in and said, "Yeah, I know all about their stupid little play to pick up women."

"Yeah, anyway. I didn't know that they were a team until right before Feelow was killed. I'd never gotten a good look at him in the alley so I didn't realize it was the same man. I felt like I owed Marcus for saving me and so I stuck around and ended up catching feelings when I caught him in the act with another bitch. I made him give me a spot on his crew as compensation but when I asked for that spot, I didn't know I was pushing others out of it. Marcus started grooming me and pretty soon, I had the street knowledge I needed to ride with the best of them."

Keisha sat there and listened intensely while I continued to tell the story, "I found out that Feelow and Marcus had some type of beef but I didn't know the extent of it, however, when Marcus' mom called him and told him that Feelow had her at gunpoint, I knew then the seriousness of what they were going through. I was with Marcus when he went to his mother's house and helped him carry Feelow out." I could see the tears as they formed in Keisha's eyes and knew that there would be more to come. I continued, "Marcus drove to some abandoned warehouse and when he got Feelow inside, he started beating him and kicking him in the body and face with his boots. He finally ended up shooting him in the head."

"Oh my God. I mean I knew they had beef but at one point, I thought they'd made up. I really thought that having Khalif would bring them closer but Marcus took Feelow before he could even meet his son," her tears fell freely and I could see the hurt that talking about Feelow caused but I couldn't do anything to stop her from hurting. She then asked, "So why didn't you let Marcus take the fall for what he'd done? Why would you give up your whole life for him?"

I replied, "I told you, I felt like I owed him for saving me in the alley that day. I knew that if he was convicted of that murder, he would be sent away for the rest of his life, but I would only get a small amount of time. I really thought that he would stick by me and make sure I was okay but that bastard didn't even thank me. He let me sit in there all these years and never once reached out."

"Damn Krystal, I'm so sorry, I've been so angry at you all this time and I didn't even know you. I finally had to pray and ask God to give me the strength to forgive you, at least for my son's sake and then I recently found out that you didn't even do it," she started to cry and I got up so I could go to where she sat. I pulled her into me and let her release all she felt.

"It's alright Keisha, you had no other choice but to be mad and hate me because you couldn't have known the truth," I said to her and then she pulled back from me.

"You don't understand, I've had Feelow's son looking up to Marcus because he was the closest thing he's had to a father. My God, I'm a piece of shit for disrespecting Feelow's memory like that. I don't even know how to tell my son."

No sooner than she said it, a small boy with eyes and a face like Feelow's walked in and stated, "Tell me what."

***

"Hello, is this Mr. Marcus Newsome?" The caller asked when I answered.

"Yeah, who the hell is this and why are you calling me by my government?"

"Mr. Newsome, this is the county medical center and I'm sorry to inform you, but your wife didn't make it. We need you to come by and sign some papers so arrangements can be made for her."

I was at a loss for words and just sat there with the phone to my ear while the lady on the other end called my name, "Mr. Newsome, sir, are you still on the line?"

I finally replied, "Um, yeah yeah I'm still here, Um, yeah I'll stop by as soon as I can," I threw my phone in the passenger seat of my car and leaned my head on the steering wheel. I had forgotten that Markill had run into the store until I heard the passenger side door open. He jumped in and asked while he held my phone in his hand, "Aye dad, you alright?"

I raised my head up and turned to look at him, but I didn't have to say a word because he sensed what was wrong.

"Mom's gone, ain't she?" He asked while his child-like voice cracked.

I nodded my head and leaned over the console so I could hold him while he cried. He truly was a momma's boy and I knew that he would never be the same. Killisha dying was my karma for all I had done and wished that I'd been more cautious and protected her better. It had always been said that you reap what you sow and it had rung true.

"It's gonna be okay son, we gon' be aight. We still got each other and we gotta stay strong for our momma," I said to him but I wasn't sure if I believed it myself.

I had to stop by the hospital but thought it would be best if I didn't take Markill with me. I wanted him to remember his mom the way she was. I stopped by our house and packed him a small bag and took him to an older couple's house down the street that Killisha had befriended. They had always treated us like family and if one didn't know better, you'd think that Markill was their grandson. They were very understanding of the situation and told me to take as much time as I needed. I hated to leave him at a time like that but I thought it would be best for the both of us. "I'll be back for him soon, I just need a couple of days," I said to them and hoped that I was telling them the truth.

I drove to the hospital so I could handle the arrangements for the woman I had loved for most of my life. I walked in and got the information for where I needed to go. When I got downstairs to the morgue, a chill came over me and it wasn't because of the temperature in the hall. "I know baby, I'm gonna miss you too," I said out loud and walked into the room that they had Killi in.

I could see the silhouette of her body underneath the sheet and felt sick to my stomach. When I got closer to the cold metal she laid upon, I nodded my head at the coroner and he pulled the sheet back. I tried my best to appear hard because my pride didn't want the next man to see me in a weakened state. I ran a finger over the side of her face and said, "Don't worry baby, I'ma take care of Markill and never let him forget you. I'm so sorry that you had to pay for my sins and I hope you can forgive me. I love you and no one will ever take that place you hold in my heart. See ya when I get there." I felt a tear slide down my cheek; as soon as I turned around, I wiped it away and walked out.

I stopped at the nurse's station to sign some paperwork and the doctor that had been taking care of Killisha walked up and asked, "Mr. Newsome, did your wife have any enemies that you know of?"

I looked at him crazy and asked, "The fuck you ask me some shit like that for?"

He pulled me to the side so no one could hear him and said, "Mr. Newsome, someone pulled the plug on your wife. You may want to find out who's responsible. Have a good day sir and I'm sorry for your loss."

I stood there frozen and thought about what he'd said but I didn't have to find out anything because I already knew who was responsible. However, I wish it would have been me instead of Killi because I wasn't sure how I was going to live without her. I was exhausted and instead of going out to look for Krystal, I decided to call it a night. However, there was no way I could go home and sleep in the bed that I had shared with Killi. I would worry about something to change into when I got up the next day. I needed time to mourn so I could get my head together for the sake of my son.

I had picked up something to eat on the way to the hotel but found myself unable to eat it. My mind and heart were too fucked up, so I got undressed and hopped in the shower instead. When I got out, I lay back in the bed and lit a spliff. About thirty minutes later, I was high as a kite. I tried to close my eyes so I could get some rest but the sounds of pleasure coming from the room next to me made it hard to do.

***

I went back to where I'd had Tammy stashed just to make sure that shit was all good. I was worried that Trap might have told Marcus where I had taken her and the fact that she was still alive.

When I stormed in and saw her sleeping peacefully, I breathed a sigh of relief.

I woke her up and said, "Aye Tammy, come on baby, I need you to get up and pack your shit. I gotta move you to another location."

She opened her eyes and looked at me disappointingly and said, "Really Terrance, is this how I'm going to have to spend the rest of my life because if it is, I think I'd rather you just go ahead and kill me like you were hired to do." I kissed her on the lips and rubbed a finger over one of her nipples and said, "Girl you know you don't wanna die and miss out on all this good dick you be getting, so get your ass up."

She laughed and reached down to rub my manhood but I grabbed her hand and said, "Uh uh. I'll give it to you real good when I get you to where we're going."

She asked, "Mmm, Are you gonna long stroke this pussy for me daddy?" She asked.

"Yo damn right, I am, and the sooner we get outta here, the sooner I'm gonna be deep in them guts."

I slapped her on her bare ass and got up so I could help her gather her things. She didn't have much at that time, so it only took us about ten minutes to get it all, and then we were on our way.

I pulled up to the Sheraton Inn and got us a room on the second floor in the very back of the hotel. We gathered what we had brought and went into the nicely furnished room. "Hopefully, you'll be able to chill here for a minute. I plan on finding a house out in the country so you can hang outside and shit. I want you to be comfortable, so just bare with me baby, okay!

"Terrance, I appreciate what you're doing but I can't live like this forever. I'm miserable. I mean I'm not miserable with you but not being able to go outside and do anything is very depressing. There has to be another way."

I felt bad for Tammy and knew that the only way to change things was to either kill her or Marcus and honestly, I didn't want to do either one. "Look, there is no other way. You saw too much and if your ass would have kept your damn mouth shut and not said anything to Keisha, we wouldn't be going through this shit."

"I know, but shit, I was just tired of her always one-upping my ass. I had genuine feelings for him but that bastard gave her a son and used me to get to her, now that bitch is shitting on his memory by fucking Marcus and letting him play daddy to Feelow's kid. That's fucked up that she would do him, like that. Shit, when he got killed, I had to turn to the fucking pipe to heal my broken heart but that bitch turned to the enemy."

"Look Tammy, I know your ass is bitter about what happened but it's time to move on and I can help you with that. Shit, I got something right here that you can catch genuine feelings for, so what's up?" I grabbed my dick and walked up to her and she looked up at me innocently and smiled.

"Hmmm, how you know a bitch ain't already got feelings for that mother fucker? That dick's so good, it made me lay down the pipe."

"Oh yeah, it's that good to you baby?"

"Mmm Hmm, I don't crave crack anymore because now I crave this dick."

"Well, won't you shut your ass up and get this mutha fucka right."

"Nigga, you ain't said shit."

Tammy pushed me back on the bed and tore my clothes off and then took hers off too. She bent over and sucked the head of my dick into her mouth. "Shit, yeah Tammy. Make a nigga see how much he means to you. Damn baby, that feels good." I put a hand on the back of her head and pushed down while she deep-throated the beast between my legs. She grabbed my nut sack and softly massaged it at the same time. I could feel myself about to cum but I wanted them seed to be fertilized deep inside of her pussy instead of wasted going down her throat. I pushed her back and said, "Nah, we ain't losing them babies today, so lay that ass down. A nigg trying to make an heir to his throne."

"Oh yeah. I think I like the sound of that," She said with a smile and lay back on the bed. I lifted her legs over my shoulders and pushed my dick in as deep as it would go.

"Yeah Terrance. Mmm yeah, fuck me good Terrance, Oh God you feel so good inside of me. Yes." She cried out as I went in and out of her.

I had gained mad respect for Tammy because once I pulled her from the streets, she stopped getting high even though she would have had an unlimited supply. She had told me, "That's not who I am but I was lost and because of you, I found myself again." And she hadn't gotten high since.

I was dicking Tammy down so good that she got a little louder than usual, "yeah, yeah Tag, Oh my God, fuck me harder baby, yeah make this pussy cum mmm."

She had gotten so loud that it made me slow my pace and say, "Damn girl, I know this dick good to you but you gotta quiet down. Shit, you so loud I bet the person in the room next door can hear your ass."

***

Tetris pulled up in the yard and had us on edge. He had never shown up like that, so his visit couldn't have been just a friendly stop. I met him at the door and said, "Sup Tetris? What brings you down this way?"

He looked at me through black soul's eyes and said, "Don't play fucking stupid. You know just why the fuck I'm here. Where the hell is my niece at?"

I opened the door further so that he could walk inside. Tetris always rode with an entourage who would take a bullet for him in a minute but I didn't think that there was anyone dumb enough to try him. Two of his men stayed outside and guarded the door but his main man Rocky came inside with him. Tetris never had to bust his own gun because he had plenty of power behind him.

Tetris passed me and went straight to the living room where Swag was waiting. I looked at her and could tell that she was scared as hell, and reminded myself that I had never seen her scared of anything.

Tetris stood six five but when he was in front of you, he seemed to be taller. His stance was very intimidating even to those who called themselves family.

"Sup unc? What are you doing my way?" Swag asked him.

"I was in the neighborhood and decided I'd just swing on by and pick up my money. How do you feel about that?"

Swag looked from Tetris to me but wasn't shit I could say to save her. "Uh, well we ain't picked it up yet but if you ..."

Tetris cut off her words and exclaimed, "If I what? Huh? How dare you disrespect me by lying in my face. I'm fucking good to you and you wanna repay me by lying. I give you my shit ten G's cheaper than other mutha fuckas and yet you can't keep it fucking real with me."

"I, I can explain."

"Nah, save that shit. I don't need you to tell me any more lies. Besides, I already know everything. I know how you come to pick up my shit and detour on the way back. Look what chasing pussy got your ass. You didn't even have the decency to let me know what was up. You were just gonna let me sit back and think shit was kosher on this end. Who the fuck do you think you dealing with? I'm not these small-time chumps you been down here fucking with. I've worked hard to build up what I have and I'm not about to let you fuck it up."

"But we know who did it and with your power behind, us we can go take that shit back."

"Oh, yo mean by starting a fucking war? I've been doing this a long time and never had to go to war with anybody. That's the shit that gets you caught up. You're supposed to keep peace in this business even when it comes to your enemies. Your father and I did our best to teach you the ropes so that one day you could possibly take over the empire but you didn't listen, which means that you've learned nothing. You wanted to be in a man's game but you couldn't even man up enough to choose business over pleasure. You let some pussy distract you. I don't need people like you on my team because in the end, you will only bring me beef and cause me misery. Now, I'll be expecting my money by the end of the week and if you don't show up with it, I will come back and family or not, you don't want me to do that."

Swag started to say something but Tetris turned his back to her and walked out. I knew that his threats were to be taken seriously and I only hoped that Swag understood that.

"Shit. I can't believe this. How the hell did he find out about this? Nobody knows but us and the mutha fuckers that pulled it off." She stated with a look of despair in her eyes.

I thought about all that Tetris said and he was right. In a game like the one we played, business should always come before anything else. Tetris was a smart man and not telling him about the robbery got us cut off, and I wasn't sure where we'd pick back up from. Once we paid Tetris his money, it would put a big dent in our sack and with Tag out there playing Captain Save a Hoe, we were even weaker.

I looked at Swag and asked, "So what are your plans now?"

She put her hands on her hips and said, "man, I'm sorry Echo. I fucked up dawg. I don't know what we're gonna do. My uncle has been my connect from the beginning, so I've never ventured anywhere else. I don't know man"

"Shit, aight, I'm going to get a hold of Tag and tell him that he needs to come back so we can get this bread together."

"And then what?" Swag asked.

"Well, your uncle said that he was done with you but that doesn't mean that I can't still deal with him."

"So, what the fuck you gonna do? Your ass gonna try to slide in my spot?" She asked with a unit on her face.

"Your spot? Bitch, you don't have a spot anymore and since someone's going to have to take it, I might as well put my application in."

Chapter Eleven

I woke up early the next morning with Killisha heavily on my mind. I couldn't believe that I would bury her so soon. I thought we had a lot of time left together. I knew that I had to get myself together for Markill's sake. My son would need me now more than ever before. I had caused Killisha to be taken away by the sins that I'd committed. Deep down, I knew that I deserved the karma coming at me but it was hard to accept.

When Ditto had first pulled me off the street, I told myself that I wouldn't be the same as other niggas out there in the game and I wasn't the same. I felt like I was worse than them. I finally sat up on the floor. I heard the couple in the next room as they got one in but they were a little quieter than they had been the night before. It reminded me of the days I had made love to my wife, and it also made me feel the pain I'd caused her heart when she caught me with other women. I didn't deserve a woman like Killisha and I felt like that's why God took her from me, even though he'd had a little help. I knew I had to get myself together, so I stood up and walked to the bathroom so I could take a hot shower. The water ran down my face and disguised the tears as they fell from my eyes. My whole world had been turned upside down but I had to move on. I was angrier than ever and was determined to find Krystal and make her pay for what she'd done. She may not have been the reason for Killi being lain up in a hospital but she was damn sure the reason she had passed so suddenly.

I got out of the shower and dried off and then got dressed. I was on a mission to make those responsible for interrupting my life pay for what they'd done. My first stop would be to see Keisha. That bitch was going to pay. I couldn't believe she'd let Krystal take the fall for the accident. I hoped that when I got there, Khalif wouldn't be home but if he was and got in my way, that lil nigga would get it too. After that, I would hit the streets and find the white bitch who changed my life forever.

Corey Robinson

I pulled some money out of my pocket and laid a bill on the counter as a tip for whoever came in and cleaned up behind me, and then I walked out and ran straight into an unexpected surprise.

"Tag, what's going on nigga? What the fuck are you doing here?" I asked.

"Yo Marcus, you aight dawg?"

Tag looked to be a little nervous to me and I had never seen him like that before. I wondered what was wrong, "Aye Tag, you acting a little nervous. Is everything okay with you? I mean, I see you come from next door and after all I heard going on in there last night, yo' ass should be looking like the kool-aid man."

"Uh yeah, yeah. I had run into a shorty I use to fuck with and we just made up for old times. How 'bout you man? You don't look so good yourself, what's going on?"

His question reminded me of why I had gone to the motel in the first place. I said, "Man, my girl got in a bad accident and she ain't make it out."

"What? Nigga, you talking 'bout Killisha? Dawg I'm sorry. Damn, that's the last thing I expected you t say, you gon' be okay? You need me to do anything?"

"Nah Tag, I'm good but thanks. The funeral will be the weekend so you are more than welcome to come through."

"Yeah, hell yeah. I'll be there."

"Well since we good, I'm a head out. I got some shit I need to take care of but I'll see you this weekend."

I gave Tag some dap and walked away; I could tell that he was hiding something but had no clue what it was. I decided to pull out of the hotel and backtrack after I thought he was gone. I would come back and knock on the door of the room he'd come out of. I was curious to know who would open it but I had a gut feeling that I wouldn't like what I found.

***

I had almost shit on myself when I walked out and ran into Marcus. My biggest fear was that Tammy would walk out of the room but I was thankful that she'd actually listened to me and stayed in. I made sure that I talked louder than usual so she would hear me talking to the man who had hired me to kill her. When Marcus finally left, I pretended to walk to my car but when he pulled far enough down the road, I ran back up to the room.

"Tag, what the hell was that? Oh my God, what are we gonna do?" She asked in desperation as soon as I walked in.

I could tell that she was scared as hell, so I pulled her to me and held her. I could feel her body as it shook in fear. I said, "Look, I have to go but I won't be gone long. I need you to pack up everything and be ready to move when I come back okay."

"Oh God, I can't do this anymore." She cried out, but I needed her to hang in there a little longer.

"Come on baby, I need you to trust me and just hold on. I'll make all of it disappear soon, please, just a little longer."

"Terrance, this is not going away unless you kill Marcus and since you haven't done that yet, then that means, you're not going to. All I want to know is where that leaves me. I'm not going to continue hiding out and running from place to place when that mother fucker is around. So you need to decide which one of us you're going to spare and you need to do it now."

I could understand just where Tammy was coming from and although she had expressed herself before, I knew that it would be the last time she'd tell me. I had to make a decision but I just needed a little longer. "Look, I'm going to move you one more time and I give you my word, it will be the last."

"Oh yeah. Well, you gave me your word the last time and your word apparently doesn't mean shit. I'm telling you Terrance, this is it. This is the last time and if you don't handle your business, my ass is gone."

"Okay, alright. Just let me go take care of the shit with my crew and I'll be back. This will be it, I promise."

The look in her eyes broke my heart. I didn't want to lose her the same way I lost Carla, so I made up my mind to eliminate Marcus from the equation. I would wait until after Killi's funeral so he could say his final goodbyes, and then I planned on sending his ass straight to hell. In the meantime, I needed to go check on my crew so I headed across town. I pulled up just as a black Denali pulled out. The windows were darkly tinted and made it hard for me to see inside. When I looked and saw that it was a New York license plate, I had a bad feeling.

I parked and got out but before I made it to the door, Echo walked out and met me.

"Aye Tag, I hope you back to give me that bread. Tetris just left here looking for his money. Said Swag had till the end of the week to get it to him, and he already knew about the jack," Echo said before I could get a word out.

"The fuck. How that nigga already knew that shit? Make me feel like his ass had something to do with it." I said with raised eyebrows.

"Yeah, nigga did find out mightily fast."

"So what happens now? What if he doesn't get his money? Mutha fucka don't want none of this Glock." I stated with an attitude that only a killer could possess.

"Nah man, we don't want it to come to that, but if we don't get it there, he said he's coming back to get it himself."

"Well, let his ass come back. The fuck he calls himself doing? I ain't afraid of him and his weak ass entourage. That bitch can kiss my ass, he'll get it when we can get it there." I walked away and left Echo standing there by himself. I didn't take kindly to threats. I was a killer, not a fucking pussy.

When I walked in, Swag had money going through the counting machine, getting it ready to give to Tetris. I looked at her and nodded and then proceeded to my room. I had seriously thought about putting Tammy up in the house because at least, she'd have Echo and Swag for protection when I wasn't there. The only thing that stopped me was the thought of something happening to my people. We had been through some shit together and always made it out, but I was afraid that one day we wouldn't be so lucky, and if Marcus found out that Tammy was still alive, our luck would definitely run out.

I pulled my bed away from the wall and found the slit that was on the edge of my mattress. The small key was right where I'd always put it. No one else knew of its existence and I planned to keep it that way. After I got the key, I moved my nightstand and pulled back the carpet from the wall just enough to reach the keyhole, that was between the slats on the wooden floor. It looked like a regular floor and you'd have to know the exact spot to stick the key in to open it.

Once I had it open, I pulled the boards up and pulled out a bag that contained five hundred thousand dollars. I had been saving the money so that when I retired from killer mode, I would be set. I had several bags like the one I'd pulled out but they were all in different locations. I sat it on my bed and counted out three hundred thousand. Two hundred to help out Swag and the other hundred I would give back to Marcus. It was the money he'd paid me to kill Tammy. I was going to tell him that I couldn't do it and ask him to call off the hit. I had planned on pulling out all my bags and leaving the state with Tamy. I was going to start fresh somewhere else and would assure Marcus that his secret would never get out. I just hoped he believed me because I had never made a senseless kill and didn't want him to be my first.

I secured the rest of the money back in my spot and walked out of my room. I went to the living room and placed the two hundred G's on the couch beside Swag and said, "I'm leaving town. I'll be back in a little while to get my shit."

"The fuck? What the hell are you talking 'bout Tag? What the fuck is going on?" Echo jumped up and asked.

I wanted him to know the truth so I told it, "I'm taking Tammy and we gonna go where nobody knows us and start a life together. This shit is too stressful hiding her out from spot to spot."

"And what you gonna do about Marcus?" Swag asked.

"I'm going to give him his money back and a guarantee that Tammy will never talk."

"Damn nigga, pussy that good?" Echo asked.

"I'm tired of living like this and I'm ready to settle down. Maybe plant some seeds and shit. She is the one I want to do it with."

"You sure Tag?" Swag asked with a crazy look.

"I've never been so sure of anything in my life. I want to be normal and build something with someone special. It's time man, Hell, a nigga ain't getting no younger."

"And what you gonna do if Marcus doesn't want to hear that shit?"

"Then his ass is dead," I said and walked out.

***

I pulled back into the hotel once I noticed Tag's car gone. I hoped that I could find out what he was hiding. Whoever he had been with had to still be in that room and I was determined to find out who it was. I had my gun ready to pull just in case I needed it. When I got to the room door, I knocked and waited. It took a minute for whoever was in there to open up but when they finally did, I wasn't prepared to see who looked back at me.

"Terrance, I thought you took …" Tammy said as soon as she opened the door. When she saw me, she cried out "Oh my God," and tried to close the door but I was a little faster than her.

I pushed her down on the floor and shut the door behind me and said, "well, well, well, am I looking at a ghost, or is your ass still alive?"

"Marcus please. If I was going to say something don't you think I would have done so by now? Please, I don't wanna die."

"You should have thought about that before you ran your fucking mouth to Keisha."

"I know, I know I shouldn't have said anything to her but she always thinks she knows it all. I just wanted to hurt her, that was it. I would never go to the police. If I wanted to do that I could have done years ago but I didn't. You have to give me credit for that. Please Marcus, please, I just found out I'm pregnant. Please."

I couldn't believe that Toe Tag had the bitch hidden out all that time. I paid that mutha fucka a hundred grand to eliminate the bitch in front of me and yet, she was still breathing. That nigga had snaked me and yet, had the nerve to get the bitch knocked up. Tammy's cries didn't mean shit to me, though. That bitch knew too much and I couldn't risk that one day, she would use it against me.

"I can't let you live Tammy, that shit could come back one day and bite me in my ass. I ain't going to fucking prison because of you," I said and thought back eleven years earlier. I remembered Krystal telling me that she had seen someone looking in the window but I brushed that shit off. I had wished that I'd listened and then I wouldn't be in the situation I was in. I pulled my gun out from under my shirt and screwed the silencer on the tip. Tammy began to scoot away from me but she wouldn't get very far.

She began to plead again, "Please Marcus, please don't do this."

I cocked the gun and a bullet made its way to the chamber but before I could get the trigger pulled back, I felt a presence behind me and turned around.

"The fuck you doing in here Marcus, huh?" Toe Tag asked as he pointed a gun between my eyes.

"Nigga, you told me you took care of this little problem but that bitch is still breathing. What the fuck is up with that shit?" I asked.

"She's not a problem to you Marcus. She ain't gonna say shit. She could have done that all those years ago but she didn't, so why would you think she'd go and do it now?"

"Nigga, I ain't trying to hear all that you talking. I paid you to do a job and you took my money but didn't deliver what I paid you to do. That's a bad business Tag."

Toe Tag threw the bag he had been holding down on the floor beside me and said, "It's all in there. Every single dollar."

"Bitch, you call yourself giving me my money back. Are you fucking serious? All this over her ass. When the hell did she become so important to you?"

"I couldn't kill her, Marcus. I had every intention to but I thought about my momma and about Carla, and I couldn't go through with it. I've been hiding her in different spots so you or no one else would realize it but me or her either can't live like that anymore."

"So yo think you just gon' throw my money back at my feet and shit gonna be good? What the fuck are you thinking Tag? This is what you do, you kill people for a living not spare them. She got your head fucked up like that and then you got the nerve to plant seeds in the bitch." I said and could tell by the look on his face that he didn't know she was pregnant.

He looked at Tammy but before he could say anything she said, "I found out yesterday. I snuck to the store and bought a test and it came back positive but you came back and moved me so fast that I didn't have a chance to tell you. But yes Terrance, I'm pregnant."

Toe Tag's whole demeanor changed after Tammy revealed the news. He lowered his weapon and looked up at me and said, "Marcus man, think about how you felt when you met Killi. You knew that you didn't want to spend a day without her and you would have done anything to make it happen. Then you find out she's having your seed and it was the icing on the cake. Come on man, I gave you your money back. I just need you to spare her."

Him bringing up Killi softened my heart because she was the only woman who had me tamed. When I first met her, I didn't have shit, but Killi wasn't focused on the material stuff, she was only focused on me and I did her dirty. However, she forgave me for every wrong thing I'd done against her but I still didn't stop there. I continued with my dirt and now she was gone because of it.

I looked at Tag and asked, "how can I be sure that later on down the line, she won't break and get me cased up? I don't know if I can take that chance."

"Marcus, we've been dealing with each other for a while and you gotta trust me when I tell you that your secret is safe. I'm taking Tammy and we gonna go somewhere far away from here and build a life together, and I guess now, raise a family. You know my word is good. Come on man, give me a break."

"You know Tag, I actually prayed and I told God that if he spared Killi, I'd change my ways and do right but that mutha fucka took her anyway. That shit took a lot out of me and it left my son without a mother. That shit that happened to her was all because of me and now I got to protect Markill. If that shit she knows ever gets out, them crackas are going to send me away forever. I don't think I can take that chance man." I said and raised my gun so that it pointed at Toe Tag's face.

Tag had put his gun up and made no attempt to reach for it again when I said, "Yo Tag, shorty gotta go and if I got to send you with her then so be it."

"So you gonna do it like that bruh? This is your chance right here, right now to make up for all the things you've done. You can make shit right for your seed dawg but if something happens to me, you know when Swag and Echo find out they gon' seek revenge, and when they do, I can assure you that they won't spare you or him."

"Mutha fucka, is that a threat? You think I'm worried about them bitches you roll with? Fuck you Tag. You should have stuck to the plan. You know the rules, never leave a witness breathing and since you did, now you gotta pay for it along with them."

I didn't even give him a chance to get a word out before the bullet entered the middle of his forehead, and before Tammy could get her scream out, a bullet went down her throat. Toe Tag asked for it because he knew the rules of the game and he'd made his choice. A nigga like me followed protocol because sympathy for a mutha fucka's feelings wasn't going to get me cased up. I grabbed the bag of money he dropped on the floor and went to go find the others that could put me out of commission.

Corey Robinson

Chapter Twelve

"Have you even heard from her?" Carrie asked me in a concerned voice.

I looked at her like she had two heads and replied, "nah, she ain't reached out yet."

"Yet. Oh my god B, what if she's not in a position to reach out? What if his ass had done something to her? Maybe we should go down there and make sure everything is good."

"Look Carrie, I appreciate your concern but my gut tells me that she's good, so until I feel differently, I'm not going down there to fuck up what she has going on."

"Well, I'll go then." No sooner than she said it, Jambo walked out on the back patio where we were and asked, "You'll go where?"

"I'm worried about Krystal, so I wanted to go down and check on her," She told him but Jambo shut her down quickly.

"She is very well trained, so I can assure you that she can handle what she went down there to do. Leave her be. She'll be back."

Carrie caught on instant attitude and walked inside leaving me and Jambo to ourselves.

Jambo sat in one of the patio chairs beside me. The new spot was a far cry from what we were used to but it was necessary for the time being. It was a place that no one, not even our closest comrades knew about. After we jacked the forty keys, we knew that eventually, someone would figure it out, so we relocated. I didn't think that Marcus or any of Echo's crew would be dumb enough to come for me and my people but I still played cautiously.

Jambo took a small sip of his Ciroc and asked, "you good? Seems like you got a lot of shit on your mind."

"Nah man, I'm just thinking about how I just got her back and if anything goes wrong, I could lose her all over again."

"Ya know she has been gone for a minute. We could make that trip. My girl could have a point."

I turned and looked at my right-hand man and said, "Yeah, we could show up and show out but how do you think Krys is gonna feel about that? I either trust her to do it and come back or I go against what she asked of me. I got to believe that she knows what's best, and let her handle it. If I go running after her, it will make her feel like I think she's weak and I can assure you, she's the strongest woman I know."

"Aight man, I understand what you are saying but if she ain't called or nothing, then she may not be able to."

"Look Jam, I appreciate your concern and don't get me wrong, I'm concerned too but I have to respect what she asked of me because if the shoe was on the other foot, I'd expect the same out of her. She knows that if she needs me, all she has to do is send word. Until then, I let her run it," I said angrily and got up.

I was trying to play it cool but the truth was deep down, I was losing my mind. I couldn't lose her again and if I didn't hear from her soon, I was going to go against everything my father taught and go get her myself.

***

The drive to Brooklyn was one we had to take because if we lost Tetris as our connect, it would be a minute before we could get back on our feet. We already had to come off a big lump of our bread with no product to make it back up, and with Tag out of the loop, it was just me and Swag.

We rode in silence for a while and I was certain that we both had the same thoughts. We were about to take a big chance and ask Tetris to put us back on. He had been our supplier for years and we had only had that one issue and he was ready to cut us off. If I had to, I would make the pick-ups instead just so he would keep dealing with us."

"Look Swag, when we get there, just shut the hell up and let me do all the talking. Can you do that?" I asked her.

"Yo Echo, I feel like I need to speak up and say something to him. I mean, look at how I fucked up. I at least need my uncle to know that I truly am remorseful. I can't just go in there and not say shit."

"Yeah, actually you can. At least wait till I'm done talking. Shit, we need him and the last thing that needs to happen is you saying some dumb shit to fuck us up even more. I think I can talk to him and get him to keep supplying us. What the hell are we gonna do? Marcus ain't got that B-More connect anymore, Ditto's been dead and gone. That fuck nigga Stanley Earl says we don't spend enough money to move his shit, so Tetris is it. Please, just don't say nothing."

"Aight damn. But once the deal is made, I'm gonna make my peace."

I pulled up to the gate that would open to the road that led us to Tetris. I looked around and told myself that one day, I would live just like he was. However, I also knew that being in the dope game was not a secure career and could end at any time. I had seen so many who thought they couldn't be touched go down and everyone knew that to get out of the game, you either went to prison or to the grave. I saw some pull out themselves and enjoy the riches they had made but if I couldn't get Tetris to agree to put us back on, the dream of being a retired boss would never happen.

We had finally made it to the end of the long driveway and I parked the car and turned to Swag one more time and said, "we have an agreement that I do all the talking right."

"Yeah nigga damn. You don't gotta worry, I ain't gonna say shit till the deal is made. I give you my word."

"Aight, let's go, and grab that loot out of the compartment," I said and got out. I stood and waited for Swag to get the money we owed Tetris out of the stash spot. When she pulled it out, she handed it to me but I pushed it back and said, "Nah T, I think you should be the one to hand him the bag." and then I turned and proceeded to walk up to the house with her close behind me.

Tetris' two goons stood at the bottom of the steps that led to the porch. We nodded to them in acknowledgement and walked up. The front door was huge and trimmed in gold accents, that nigga was living it up and I knew that the money we brought him was only pocket change compared to what he was used to. I couldn't understand why Swag didn't do the right thing because if she did, everything Tetris owned would have been hers once he stepped away from the rush.

"Damn Swag, I ain't know Tetris was living this fucking large. This is what I want one day and I ain't stopping till I get it," I said while I continued to look around.

"Man, this shit don't mean nothing. Hell, all of it could be taken away in one swoop."

Before I had a chance to knock on the door, it opened up and a fine-ass red bitch with some boy shorts and a tank top smiled at me and said, "Hello Echo. Swag. Tetris is expecting you, and you'll find him out back by the pool. Follow me."

"Dayuum," I exclaimed, "Bitch, you ain't tell me about all this. Remind me to beat your ass when we get back home."

I followed behind the red bone and watched as her ass cheeks jiggled with each step. I noticed a small tattoo on her right shoulder that said, "Spoiled" and for some reason, it made me smile.

She led us to a set of gold-trimmed sliding glass doors and then pushed them open. When we walked through, I saw Tetris as he sat beside the pool in a lounge chair with a blunt, in his hand and another half-naked bitch in his lap. The girl that had led us to him bent down and sucked his bottom lip into her mouth and once she let it go, she said, "Your company is here baby."

Tetris reached his hand around her and squeezed an ass cheek and said to the one on his lap, "Yall go get the bed warmed up and ready, I'll be up in a little bit."

She replied, "Okay daddy, but don't take too long because you know we don't mind getting started without you." She smiled and stood and when she did, she kissed the red bone and then grabbed her hand and the two of them walked away.

My dick was rocked the fuck up and there was no way I could hide it. Tetris noticed and said, "it's all good. I'd be more worried if they didn't have that effect on you.

I know you mean no disrespect. Now grab a seat and let's talk."

Swag and I each grabbed a chair and no sooner than we sat down, a white girl with a bikini bottom on and no top came out with a tray in her hand. She sat it down on the table and then leaned over and ran a hand over Tetris' bare chest, and then walked back the way she had come.

He raised an eyebrow and pointed to the tray that held blunts, weed, cocaine and rolled up hundred dollar bills and said, "Enjoy yourself. I always like my guests to be relaxed during business."

I had never really gotten into the cocaine thing but I decided to try a line just so he didn't feel insulted. As soon as I inhaled the powdered substance, my nose felt like it was on fire. "Holy shit. That shit's potent as fuck," I said while I held my head back.

Tetris replied, "Yes, indeed it is. It's pure Peruvian Flake. No cut and sure to keep your dick hard for hours. You'll be glad you tried it because I have a special treat for you. Now let's get down to business."

Swag handed Tetris the bag of money and said, "It's all there unc."

He opened the bag and then called out, "Mel, come take care of this for me." I looked to see who he had called Mel and saw a dark-skinned goddess appear. Her baby-making hips were wide and swayed like a runway model when she walked. She had on a white lace see-through bodysuit and nothing else. I scanned down her whole body but what caught my eye was how the fabric formed the outline of her pussy lips. It had been a minute since I'd fucked and I hoped that the special surprise he had planned for me included a pussy as fat as hers was.

The woman he called Mel grabbed the bag and then turned to me and smiled. Her dimples were so deep; I was sure that I could drink from them. I appreciated all flavors but a dark-skinned hottie like the one in front of me could get the rest of them hoes canceled. "Damn," I said out loud when she turned and walked away.

Tetris smiled and said, "When we're finished, you can find her upstairs waiting for you."

"Look Tetris, you and I are both businessmen and want the same things out of life," I said to him but before I could continue, he cut me off.

Tetris asked, "and what exactly is it that you say we both want?"

"To make enough money and live long enough to retire from the madness. However, you are much closer to your goal than I am. I'm trying to get on your level but I need you to help me out so I can."

Tetris nodded his head and said, "Continue on Echo and stop beating around the bush. Tell me what you want."

"I want you to put us back in business. I know that Swag fucked up but we managed to bounce back from it. You got what you were owed and the jack really only affected us. You lost nothing. However, because of the jack, we're out on our ass and need you to pull us up."

"And you'll get the funds from where to pay for my product?"

"Well, I was hoping we could get it on consignment again but this time, I will be the one making the pick-ups and drop-offs instead of your niece."

Tetris raised an eyebrow and leaned forward. He looked from me to Swag but right before he spoke, his phone rang.

"Yeah," he said when he answered. He listened intensely before he spoke again, "Thanks, I'll be sure to let them know." He pressed end on his phone and told us something we were not ready to hear, "They found your friend ya know, the assassin. I'm sorry to inform you but he is no longer breathing."

***

I picked up Markill from the older couple's house and together we went home. Killisha's funeral would be held the next day and I needed to make sure I and my son were prepared. Markill was silent and I knew that he was still mourning the loss of his mother. I asked him, "Aye son, how do you feel?"

He turned to me with sad eyes and said, "I'm good, dad. It's just going to be strange not having her around. I miss her already."

"Yeah, me too but we gon' get through this together. Ya know she wouldn't want us down here all sad and shit. Let's just always keep her memory alive. Okay."

"Okay dad."

We got out of the car and walked into the home that felt empty. There were no smells coming from the kitchen like before but the sweet smell of Killi was still lingering as if her presence were still there. Markill ran off to his room while I sat on the couch and reminisced about the days before I knew that me or Markill either one would never be the same and I knew that he needed me more than ever.

I had drifted off to sleep and when I opened my eyes, I realized that it was a new day. I jumped up off the couch and went to my son's room. When I didn't find him there, I went and checked mine and Killis' room and as soon as I opened the door, I saw Markill asleep on his mother's pillow. I walked in and sat on the bed beside him and rubbed his back until he woke.

He looked at me through sleepy eyes and said, "I don't wanna go say goodbye to her dad. Can I just stay home?"

I replied, "Come on son. You gotta do this for her. Don't you think it's gonna break her heart to look down and not see her favorite little person in the world? You were her everything and she needs you there so that way, she can rest in peace so come on."

Markill didn't reply but instead got up and went to his room to prepare to say goodbye to his queen.

When we walked out of the house, something in my gut made me feel like it would be my last time there. I knew that Krystal was out to get me but I honestly didn't feel like she would be able to kill me. I had always known how she felt about me, so killing me would be hard for her. However, I'd play along with her and pretend to be scared until our paths crossed again.

When I and my son made it to the funeral home, there were numerous people there that I was not familiar with. Trap was there but Creep refused to come. He said it was a bad omen to attend a funeral but he would send his condolences.

I walked up to Trap and asked. "Who in the hell are all these people?"

He replied, "They say they use to work with her but them mutha fuckas acting like they too good to sit on the side with us street niggas."

"Hmm, fuck 'em we are here for Killisha."

I acknowledged everyone in attendance and when the funeral began, me and Markill sat on the front row. I stared at the open casket as Killi lay there motionless. She looked like an angel and I knew that God would take her under his wings and keep her safe for me. I wasn't sure if heaven was the place I'd go once I was eliminated from the earth, so I took in as much of her beauty as I could just in case I'd never see her again because I could very well go in the opposite direction.

The reverend that presided over it called me up so that I could say my final words of love about the woman that I would miss so much.

"Um, I didn't prepare myself to speak today because honestly, I wasn't sure I'd be able to handle it. However, I couldn't let God take her until I made my peace. Killisha came into my life when I was a nobody and made me feel like I was everything. She stuck by me when no one else would and gave me the greatest gift I ever could have received, our son. I did a lot of things and broke her heart several times and yet, she loved me through it all. There's no way I could ever replace her and wouldn't even know how to begin to try. I asked God to spare her and take me instead but I guess He was ready for His angel back. I just hope that Killisha knows how much she meant to me. I will raise our son in the way that she would have and hope it makes her proud. There is not a person alive who sacrificed as much for me as she had, and I will forever be grateful to her. Killisha may leave us physically but her memory will remain with us forever. Thank you."

All of a sudden, the sound of someone clapping came from the back of the church. I looked up while everyone else turned their heads and looked back. A figure appeared in all black and said, "Bravo Marcus, you almost had me convinced."

***

There would have been no way I'd have missed the funeral. I had to attend and see just how Marcus would grieve. And although I wasn't responsible for the death of the woman that lay in the open casket, I felt pure satisfaction by her being there. Marcus deserved to suffer and the nerve of him to say that the bitch had sacrificed more for him than anybody made me wanna spit on her corpse.

When he was done with his speech, I clapped at his performance and when all eyes turned to me the same way they had all those years ago in the courtroom, I stood and said, "Bravo Marcus, you almost had me convinced."

The gasps from the other attendants were loud but brought a smile to my face. These people didn't know me or the shit I gave up for the liar at the front of the room.

Marcus said, "Please Krystal, not here."

"Why not Marcus? Don't you think this place is as good as any other? Oh, you don't want these people here to know how I gave up my life for you and you shitted on me like it was nothing, and then you got the nerve to stand at the front of a church and before God and say that she sacrificed more for you? Huh Marcus?"

"Please, could you just have some respect if not for me, do it for my son.;" He pleaded and grabbed his child.

I looked down at the little boy and wondered what our child would have looked like if he would have allowed me to have it and said, "Really, you ask me to respect the child you bore with her when you totally disrespected the one we made together. Remember that child Marcus? Yeah, kid, you would have had a brother or sister your same age but your daddy made me kill it."

The tears started to form but I closed my eyes to stop them from falling. When I opened them back up, Trap stood in front of me.

"Krys, come one. I know how he did you was fucked up but don't do this to yourself."

He pulled me close to him and I didn't even try to stop it. I needed the comfort he was giving me so I welcomed it.

"Come on. Let me get you out of here," Trap said.

I nodded and looked up at Marcus one more time and said, "I'm a leave and let you finish burying your dead wife but you will see me again. I give you my word."

Trap walked me out of the chapel and to the taxi that waited for me. I didn't want to drive to the funeral because I honestly didn't feel that I was stable enough to do so.

"Hey man, you can push on. Here's some ends for your trouble but I got it from here," Trap said and passed the taxi driver some cash. He then turned to me and said, "Come on. I'll take you where you gotta go."

I followed Trap to his car and got in but said nothing. I knew that I was wrong to bust in on the funeral but at that moment, I didn't give a fuck about anyone else's feelings but mine. My only intention was to hurt Marcus and whoever happened to get in the way of that would have to suffer with him.

It was quiet in the car but Trap finally broke the silence, "Yo, I ain't neva seen yo act like that before. What the fuck happened to you?"

"I suffered for something Marcus did and that bastard left me for dead. Yeah, I chose to do it but he could have done right by me. You know the story, Trap."

"Come on Ma, you gonna let that mutha fucka change who you are? That fucking bitterness you harboring gon' eat your ass up. Let that shit go."

"That's easier said than done. Do you know what the hell I went through? Huh? Look at my fucking wrists. Look at 'em dammit." Trap cut his eyes over at me and when he did, I turned my arms over so he could see the scars and then I said, "That's what Marcus did to me. That mother fucker made me want to kill myself and every time I tried, them bitches saved me, over and fucking over again. I didn't want to come out of there because the only person I had didn't have me. I saved his ass from going to prison. You know they would have sent his black ass away for life if it wasn't for me. He would have had to raise his little bastard from behind those prison gates, but I went for him instead because my dumb white ass actually thought that he would be there for me. His ass moved on though, like what I did didn't mean shit, so fuck him, his dad bitch and his bastard son. He will pay for what I went through and you or no one else is going to prevent that."

I breathed a heavy sigh of relief because it had felt so good to get the words I'd held in my heart out. I knew that Trap had been one of the few good guys on Marcus' crew and I knew he'd understand just where I was coming from. However, no matter how good of a person he was, he couldn't heal the pain I held inside of me. The only way I would get over it was to give Marcus what he truly deserved.

"Krys, look, I'm sorry that you went through that shit alone but do you really think that Marcus is worth taking a risk of going back to prison for?"

"Going back? Hell no, that's not going to happen. I don't plan on killing him, besides, I'm sure there are plenty others who would like that pleasure. I just want him to feel my pain. I want him to know how it feels to sacrifice for the one you love only for them to shit on your ass. Marcus taught me everything I know and I just want him to see how well it paid off."

***

I couldn't believe that Krystal came into the church like that and disrespected Killi's memory. I would have rather she killed me than do that shit. I knew that she was pissed because of what she sacrificed for me but it was her dumb ass that fessed up. I didn't hold a gun to her head and make her do it.

After Krystal had left with Rap, all eyes turned to me for an explanation but I didn't owe them mutha fuckas anything, Markill would be the only one I'd answer to.

"Look son, I know what happened in there had you confused, so I'm gonna tell you about it. That woman was someone your pops use to fuck with. I ain't gonna lie to you and tell you she was nobody to me because she was. Ya momma knew about her, she just didn't know about your mom. Some shit happened, some real bad shit and your uncle Feelow was killed. I know all this time you have been in the blind about that but I killed him because of his disloyalty. Well, Krystal took the fall for it so I wouldn't go to prison and instead of riding with her, I forgot about her and continued on with life while she suffered for my sins, and now she wants payback."

He looked at me confused, "So you did kill Khalif's daddy? I thought he was your friend."

"Son, in the game I'm in, it's those closest to you that stab you in the back. You know the saying "keep your friends close and your enemies closer." Take heed to that shit because it's true hood knowledge. Feelow was trying to take me out so he could take over. He had your G'ma at gunpoint and would have killed her if I didn't stop him. He had lost his fucking mind and was only getting worse. I had to kill him, if not he would have got me instead."

"So the lady that came in the church took the blame so you wouldn't have to go to prison? Why didn't you stick by her dad? If she gave up everything for you, why did you turn your back on her? You told me to always ride with those who are loyal to me but you weren't even loyal yourself."

Markill was only a child and yet had the knowledge of a grown man. I was glad that he'd listened all those times I preached hood facts to him. I knew that he would one day be successful in the game and it made me very proud.

"Yeah, I was wrong. I do admit that. That white bitch had my back at all corners and I did her dirty, but I'm gonna go find her and try to make shit right between us."

Markill asked, "Are you going to kill her dad?"

I looked at him and lied, "Nah son. I'm going to spare her. She's given up enough for me already. I'm just going to call a truce so we can squash this beef."

I told him the lie so easily and hoped that he believed it. I swung by the older couple's house and dropped Markill off and said, "I'm going to go take care of this and I'll be back to get you when I'm done. Okay."

"Okay dad, I'll be waiting for you, but please don't be gone long."

"I won't son. I promise I'll be back," I just hoped I was telling him the truth.

Corey Robinson

Chapter Thirteen

"The fuck you mean Tag is no longer breathing," I asked as soon as the words came out of Tetris' mouth.

"I was just informed that he was found along with a female by the name of Tammy Watson. They each had a bullet hole between their eyes. Any ideas of who could have done it?" Tetris replied.

Swag said, "Yeah. I got an idea and his ass gonna have to pay for that shit."

I sat up in the chair that I had sat in and put my head down in the palms of my hands. Toe Tag was a hired assassin and had never slipped up, so for him to be killed instead, he had to have called a truce and then relaxed his gun only to be turned on and killed himself.

I already knew that it was Marcus who pulled the gun on him. He had to have found out that Tag hadn't killed Tammy like he said he did. "Dammit, I knew that shit was going to backfire on his ass," I exclaimed and stood up. "I'm a kill Marcus ass myself. That muthafucka could never be forgiven for that shit."

"Man, I can't believe Tag is really gone. The fuck we gonna do without him? He was our fucking brother, man. That shit ain't right man, that shit just ain't fucking right," Swag exclaimed with tears in her eyes. I had never seen Swag bitch up until that moment. She had always played hard but the thought of never seeing Tag again broke her inner core.

Tetris let us have a moment of silence so that we could absorb what he had just revealed and then said, "I think our business here should be postponed until you take care of your little problem. Obviously, you have a beef that needs to be squashed."

"Nah Tetris, we can handle that shit and still be on point. We need that shipment to keep us on our feet," Swag stated.

"I will not give you my product in the middle of a street beef that you have going on. As of now, you are a liability because you seek revenge on someone you once fucked with. I will not take a chance of losing out, so when you handle your little problem, you can check back with me then. Until that happens, forget you even know me. My men will show you out." Tetris said and got up. He walked away and left me and Swag standing there looking dumbfounded. A couple of minutes later his two bodyguards walked up on us. They didn't even have to speak because the look in their eyes spoke for them.

I held my hands up in surrender and said, "yeah, yeah we know," and then I and Swag walked back through the house and out front where we had parked. I realized that Tetris had taken such a long time to call the deal because he had waited to make sure we didn't have other shit going on. The news of Tag's death rocked our souls way more than it did his.

When we got in the car, Swag asked, "So what the fuck are we gon' do now?"

I looked at her and said, "We bout to knock Marcus off the mutha fuckin map."

***

I pulled up to the complex that Keisha lived in and sat there for a moment. I knew that my time on earth was limited but I wasn't sure that I was ready to go yet. When I first got in the game, I was a good person but I let the riches and the bitch's change who I was. I had done people dirty over the years and had made enemies that I knew would one day come after me. However, I never thought that it would be Killisha who paid my debt. I had to avenge her death, so I decided to start with the person who'd caused the accident in the first place and then I'd work my way down from there. I knew earlier when I'd dropped Markill off that it may be the last time I saw him. I knew that he was in good hands if something did happen because the couple loved him almost as much as me and his mom.

I pulled my gun out and made sure that the clip was full of ammo. I screwed the silencer on the tip and then stared out of the front window. I needed to make sure that no one was around lurking because I didn't need to be identified. I no longer had someone who would have my back and be willing to take that ride to prison in my place, so I had to be careful.

I finally got out of my ride and walked up the stairs to the apartment Keisha and Khalif lived in. I hoped that Khalif was asleep and didn't hear me because I didn't want to make him a victim too. However, I wasn't beyond taking his heartbeat along with his mother's. The lights were out in all the apartments but I knew that all closed eyes weren't asleep, so I pulled the hoodie over my head and kept my gun in my pocket so it wouldn't be seen.

When I got to Keisha's door, I turned the knob and it opened. I knew that Keisha had a bad habit of leaving her door unlocked and now it would cost her. The apartment was eerily quiet when I walked in. The only sounds came from the kitchen sink where the faucet dripped at a slow speed. Keisha had asked me weeks ago if I would come over and fix the leak for her but other things got in the way of me pulling through.

I walked slowly through the apartment until I got to Khalif's bedroom door. I opened it carefully so he wouldn't hear me and wake up. I peeked in and noticed that Khalif wasn't in his bed. I figured he was probably in bed with Keisha and felt bad because that meant he was going to have to go too.

I left Khalif's room and went straight to Keisha's only to find it empty too. I opened her closet and saw that it had been cleaned out, "Dammit Keisha, where the fuck you at?" I asked out loud. I walked back into the living room and sat on the couch for a minute so I could think about my next move, and that's when I noticed the note that lay on the coffee table. I picked it up and read it in the dimly lit room.

Keisha knew I'd come back so she wrote, "Marcus, I had to do the right thing and get Khalif out of this neighborhood. I don't want him to grow up and be a product of the streets like you and his father. He deserves a better life than that. I thought about all you told me and although it broke my heart to know that you would take something so sacred from me, I do understand why. I know the code of the streets and Feelow had broken all the rules. I was mad at you when you first told me but I have found it in my heart to forgive you. My son needs you in his life and you have always been the closest thing to a father he has. I am willing to put aside all the wrong just so Khalif can have a normal life. I am leaving you our new address so you can know where to find us. I am sorry about Killisha and pray that you and Markill get through it okay. I'll be waiting to hear from you. I hope to see you soon. Love always, Keisha."

The note touched my heart in ways that made me feel remorseful for even thinking about killing her. I and Keisha had always been close and it was because of me that Khalif was able to be born. I had saved her from Feelow's wrath on numerous occasions. I had hoped for so long that he and I could go back to the way things were between us but his mind had already been made up. I had to kill him and I regret it every day since it happened. He was my brother and I missed the times we had shared. I put the note in my pocket and got up. I looked around the room one last time and then walked out so I could go to where Keisha led me.

Keisha had changed so much over the years. She had been a great mother to Khalif and although Markill didn't get to spend much time with her because of Killisha, he still had mad love for her. I hoped that we could get back on the right track so our sons could grow up and be the kings of the streets like me and Feelow had been at one time. I knew that Keisha was hell-bent on Khalif not being out there like that but it was what he was born to do and there was nothing she could do to stop him.

I got in my car and pulled the clip out of my gun so I could put it away. I no longer thought I would be needing it. I wanted Keisha to know that I wasn't a threat, and although, I had confessed to her about Feelow's murder, I knew that Keisha was a thorough bitch. She forgave me for killing Feelow, so the least I could do was forgive her for running Killisha off the road. Her letter had changed my plans but I would soon realize that it also changed my life.

***

I didn't mean for Khalif to walk in on my conversation with Krystals but when he did, I knew that I had to tell him what was going on. The woman he had hated for so long was sitting on the couch beside me. He looked at her with eyes like Feelow and said, "You're her. You're the lady in all the stories about my daddy's murder. Why are you here?"

"Khalif son, I need you to sit down and listen to her okay, she didn't ..."

"I know she didn't kill my daddy, I was listening when my uncle Marcus told you what he'd done. I knew he was lying when you first asked him, I felt it in my heart, "Khalif stated and then he turned to Krystal and asked, "Could you tell me what happened? I'm old enough to know the real story now. Please."

Krystal turned to me and I nodded to let her know that it was okay to tell Khalif the truth. I never wanted to taint his image of Marcus but I didn't know that it had already been done. I knew that Krystal would tell Khalif the truth so he could rest his little mind and hopefully his murderous heart.

"Khalif, your uncle Marcus and your dad were like brothers growing up and formed a bond that no one thought could be broken, but in the streets, you got to have loyalty to bring solidarity. Well, a man by the name of Ditto had your dad thinking that Marcus didn't trust him anymore and there was nothing Marcus could do to make him feel differently. Anyway, your uncle Marcus protected your dad from everyone else who wanted him dead but it still didn't repair their bond. Your dad was trying to kill him but Marcus got to your dad first."

Khalif asked, "So why did you go to prison for it? Why didn't uncle Marcus go instead?

"Ya know Khalif, as you get older, you'll meet people that touch your heart in ways that no one else can, and one day, you'll find that one person that you'll sacrifice everything for, and that person to me was Marcus. I lied for him so he could be free and live his life. He wouldn't have stood a chance in that courtroom, so I did what I had to do to save him."

"So why mad at him now if you made that choice?"

"I'm mad because I gave up my life for him and he left me for dead. Not once did he reach out to me; he didn't even have the decency to thank me for what I'd done. He just left me to sit there for over ten long years and suffer like what I'd done had meant nothing to him. There's a price you have to pay for being disloyal and I need him to pay up."

Khalif was silent for a minute and then asked, "So my daddy was disloyal and that's what made him take his life?"

I finally spoke up, "Son, your daddy was a good man and don't ever let anyone tell you differently, but somewhere along the way, his mind became corrupted and it caused him to turn against those that trusted him most. However, no matter what he'd done, your daddy didn't deserve to die. I don't want you to grow up with hatred in your heart, though, because it will eat you alive."

Khalif looked from me to Krystal and said, "I don't get no hatred in my heart, only murder and he gon' have to pay one day for what he did. His bitch already paid and now he's got to get what's coming to him."

Krystal looked at me with scrunched-up eyebrows and asked, "Khalif, what did you mean when you said his bitch has already paid."

Khalif replied, "That bitch is dead and gone and I don't feel bad about it."

"What the hell are you saying Khalif? What the hell did you do?" I asked nervously. I had a bad feeling about what he would say.

Khalif answered my question and said, "It was me. I pulled the plug on her ass and sent her straight to hell."

"Oh my God. If Marcus finds that shit out he's going to kill my son." I said to Krystal with tears in my eyes. I then turned to Khalif and said, "Go to your room son. I need to sit here and absorb what you just told me. Please just go to your room for a little while."

I wondered if Marcus had figured out that the plug had been pulled on Killisha or did he think that she succumbed to her injuries. I had left that letter on the table of our old apartment so I could lead him to where Krystal had brought us. He never would have guessed that she was with us which would have made our plan easier. I was afraid for Khalif and hoped that Marcus wouldn't find out how Killi died before he got to us. He would need someone to blame and since I was the one who caused the accident in the first place, I could very well be his only suspect.

Krystal grabbed my hand and said, "Keisha, just do as I say and everything will go right. Okay."

I nodded my head and listened to the plan she had come up with.

***

I was on my way to the address that Keisha had left. I had put my gun away before I'd left her old place but I had a funny feeling in my gut and ended up pulling over halfway there and reloading the clip. I tucked it under my leg as I drove just so it would be handy in case I got pulled over. I left the stash spot where I usually put it open just in case I had to stash it again really quickly.

I was listening to "Best Pussy" by Problem and wondered if I'd be able to talk Keisha out of some pussy while I was there. I needed to run up in something wet and warm so I could relieve all the stress that I was under. My dick got hard at the thought of her riding my shit reverse cowgirl while she played with my nutsack. That bitch knew just what to do to have a nigga hooked. If I would have known that Keisha could be tamed, I would have reconsidered and made her my girl all those years ago but instead, my homie locked it down and put a seed up in it so it would be his forever, and if I wouldn't have taken his life, he'd still have all that good pussy to himself.

I was so deep in thought that I never saw the Hummer behind me until it was too late. "Holy shit," I cried out when the Hummer slammed into me. "What the fuck?" I asked and pushed the gas a little harder, however, the faster I went, so did the vehicle behind me.

When it came up and hit me a second time, I almost ran off the road. My heart sped up and for once in my life, I was scared as hell because I didn't know who it was behind me trying to take me out. I sped up as fast as my ride would go but it still wasn't enough. The Hummer slammed into me one last time and sent me right into a tree.

I opened my eyes and it felt like every bone in my body had been broken. It hurt like hell to move but I had to get out of there somehow. I searched my pocket for my cell phone but when I pulled it out, the battery was dead. "Dammit, I gotta get the hell outta here," I said and raised up. I noticed my gun on the floorboard and picked it up right before my door was pulled open.

"Get your ass out fuck boy. What the fuck do you think was gonna happen when you killed Tag? Huh? Get the fuck out," Echo said angrily.

"Echo, come on, come on man. You know I had to. He ain't give me a fucking choice man. That mutha fucka lied to me about a bitch. I paid his ass to do a job and he ain't pull through. What the fuck was I supposed to do?" I said through the pain that came with every word I spoke.

"Nigga, you ain't have to kill him," I heard Swag as she spoke up.

I looked a little closer and saw that neither one of them was armed. I guess they felt like the impact from the crash would take me out and save them the trouble, but I was a real hood nigga and taking my life wouldn't be that easy. I wondered what their plan would be since I was still breathing.

Echo turned to Swag and said, "Come on, let's pull this pussy outta the car and beat the shit out of his ass. When we are through, we gonna catch this mutha fucka on fire. Run back up and get that gas can out the back of the ride and hurry up."

When Swag ran off, I knew I needed to go ahead and make a move so I pulled out my gun and pointed it at Echo, and before he had a chance to duck, I sent one right through his dome. I knew

Swag wouldn't have heard the shot because my silencer was on the tip of it. Wasn't nothing like a silent kill.

I knew that I had to get out of the car before Swag came back and noticed Echo lay out, "Aah shit," I cried out in pain but motivation kept me pushing. I finally made it out of the car and I could faintly hear Swag as she stepped on the leaves to come back.

I went to the other side of the car and bent down and waited until I could make my move.

"Oh shit. Echo, Nah nigga get up. Come on man, get the fuck up." She exclaimed and shook Echo but she already knew that he was gone. She looked in the car and noticed that I was gone and then backed up. She couldn't have possibly thought that I would let her get away.

I came up from the side of the car and pointed my gun at her. "Bitch, don't take another step."

"Marcus, Marcus man come on, we cool, we can just walk away and forget about all of this. I ain't gon' say shit." Swag pleaded but her pleas fell on deaf ears.

"Yeah, you want me to let you walk away so you can come back at a later time and finish what you started? That's what you want bitch? Y'all come at me like yall gon' get some straightening for killing Tag. That mutha fucka should have handled his business. Yall know the rules of the game. You should never leave a witness alive, so guess what that means homie?"

"Come on Marcus, you ain't gotta do this."

"Yeah bitch, I do," I said and put a bullet through Swags throat. I checked Echos' pocket and got the keys to the Hummer he'd run me off the road in and I also found a box of matches. I grabbed the gas can and doused both of their bodies and my car with gasoline and then struck a match. I left them to burn in their eternal hell and then ran up the small hill, jumped in the Hummer and went to my final destination.

Corey Robinson

Chapter Fourteen

I saw the headlights when the vehicle pulled into the driveway and said to myself, "Game on mother fucker." I had been waiting for that moment for a very long time. The moment when I'd be able to make Marcus pay for the sins of his past. I had told Keisha to take Khalif and go somewhere safe. I would send her a text when I finished what I'd gone there to do.

The knock on the door was next and as soon as I heard it. I pushed open on the remote. "Keisha, where you at? Girl, I see you done moved up in the world. Got remote-controlled doors and shit. Aight." He said when he entered. I listened and waited until I heard him call Keisha's name again "Keisha. Where the fuck are you at? Stop playing and bring your ass out."

I pushed secure on the remote next and the front door slammed behind him and locked. Shutters came down from the windows and covered them. I would leave Marcus no way out, he would have no choice but to take what I had for him.

"Hello Marcus," I said seductively when I came around the corner so he could see me.

"Krys. The fuck yo doing here? Where the hell is Keisha?" he asked with wide eyes.

"What's the matter Marcus, you scared to be alone with a bitch you made? Don't worry baby, I'm not going to bite. Maybe sting a little but that's about it. Ain't you glad to see me? I was gone all that time, I figured you'd miss me a little at least. Don't you want some of this fresh out of the pen pussy? Huh baby?"

Marcus finally spoke and said, "What kind of game are you and Keisha playing Krys? Where fuck is she at?"

"Keisha left because I told her I wanted your sexy black ass all to myself. You don't want to be alone with me Marcus? Come one baby, let's do it like old times."

I walked up closer to him and put a hand on his dick print and squeezed. "Mmm, that dick still on swole for a bitch like me."

Corey Robinson

"Yeah Krys, you always did know how to make this mutha fucka rise up." He said and ran a finger softly down my cheek.

I tiptoed and pulled his bottom lip into my mouth and sucked it for a minute and then sucked his tongue. When I broke the kiss I said, "Let's go to the bedroom so I can ride that big daddy like I used to. I never forgot how good you felt inside of me. I missed you so much."

I grabbed his hand and led him to the bedroom and once we got there I said, "I got something really special for you baby."

Marcus had to have known better than to think that all was good with us but he had always had a weakness for pussy, so I knew just how to lure him in. As soon as he had his back to me, I picked up the baseball bat I'd had sitting by the door and before he could block me, I swung and knocked him on his ass. I heard his kneecap snap from the force of the bat and he grabbed it and cried out in pain. "Aah shit. Krys, what the fuck are you doing?"

"What's the matter Marcus? Doesn't feel too good to be knocked down, does it?"

I held the bat up over my head and he tried to crawl away but his ass was going to take what I had for him. "Aah. Uh uh. Please. Please don't Krys. come one. I can make this shit right between us. Please, just give me a chance."

"Make it right? How? How could you possibly give me back almost eleven years of my life? How, Marcus? I gave everything up for you and all I wanted in return was for you to be there for me but you turned your ass and went the other way."

"Come on Ma. A nigga had responsibilities. If I would have rode that shit with you then, mutha fuckas might have figured that shit out. I wanted them to think you were the enemy. You know I thought about you every day though."

"Marcus, you are pathetic and you no longer have the hold over me as you once did, so your begging doesn't mean shit," I said and swung the bat again. I was sure that I'd broken half of his ribs.

164

"Aah, come on baby. Just, uh uh just give me a chance to make it right. We can start over and move on. Let's fix this shit and make it right. Don't you still get love for a nigga? Huh?"

"Marcus, the love I had for you died when you made me kill our baby. You told me that we didn't need to bring a baby into the shit we had going on and yet, you had one coming with someone else. You used me but you can't use me anymore." I raised the bat one more time and when I looked down, I locked eyes with him. I held the bat high over my head but for some reason, I just couldn't bring it down.

Marcus breathed heavily on the floor as he waited for my next move. I let a tear fall and then threw the bat across the room and said, "You were my everything Marcus but now you are nothing. My intention was to bring you here and kill you but honestly, you're not even worth a bullet. Have a nice life or better yet, death."

I turned to leave but his next question stopped me in my tracks, "Please just tell me what Killisha had ever done to you. Why did you go to the hospital and pull the plug on her?"

I raised my eyebrows and replied, "It wasn't me Marcus. I didn't pull that plug."

"Then who?" He asked.

Another voice came from behind him and said, "It was me. I pulled the plug on that bitch."

I smiled and looked into Khalif's eyes and said, "He's all yours kid," and walked out. And before I made it to the front door, a shot rang out and sent Marcus straight to hell.

The End

Lock Down Publications and Ca$h Presents assisted publishing packages.

BASIC PACKAGE $499
Editing
Cover Design
Formatting

UPGRADED PACKAGE $800
Typing
Editing
Cover Design
Formatting

ADVANCE PACKAGE $1,200
Typing
Editing
Cover Design
Formatting
Copyright registration
Proofreading
Upload book to Amazon

LDP SUPREME PACKAGE $1,500
Typing
Editing
Cover Design
Formatting
Copyright registration
Proofreading
Set up Amazon account
Upload book to Amazon
Advertise on LDP Amazon and Facebook page

***Other services available upon request. Additional charges
may apply
**Lock Down Publications
P.O. Box 944
Stockbridge, GA 30281-9998
Phone # 470 303-9761**

Corey Robinson

Submission Guideline

Submit the first three chapters of your completed manuscript to ldpsubmissions@gmail.com, subject line: Your book's title. The manuscript must be in a .doc file and sent as an attachment. Document should be in Times New Roman, double spaced and in size 12 font. Also, provide your synopsis and full contact information. If sending multiple submissions, they must each be in a separate email.

Have a story but no way to send it electronically? You can still submit to LDP/Ca$h Presents. Send in the first three chapters, written or typed, of your completed manuscript to:

LDP: Submissions Dept
Po Box 944
Stockbridge, Ga 30281

DO NOT send original manuscript. Must be a duplicate.

Provide your synopsis and a cover letter containing your full contact information.

Thanks for considering LDP and Ca$h Presents.

NEW RELEASES

KINGZ OF THE GAME 7 by PLAYA RAY

SKI MASK MONEY 2 by RENTA

BORN IN THE GRAVE 3 by SELF MADE TAY

PROTÉGÉ OF A LEGEND 3 by COREY ROBINSON

BLOOD OF A BOSS **VI**

SHADOWS OF THE GAME II

TRAP BASTARD II

By **Askari**

LOYAL TO THE GAME **IV**

By **T.J. & Jelissa**

TRUE SAVAGE **VIII**

MIDNIGHT CARTEL IV

DOPE BOY MAGIC IV

CITY OF KINGZ III

NIGHTMARE ON SILENT AVE II

THE PLUG OF LIL MEXICO II

CLASSIC CITY II

By **Chris Green**

BLAST FOR ME **III**

A SAVAGE DOPEBOY III

CUTTHROAT MAFIA III

DUFFLE BAG CARTEL VII

HEARTLESS GOON VI

By **Ghost**

A HUSTLER'S DECEIT III

KILL ZONE II

BAE BELONGS TO ME III

TIL DEATH II

By **Aryanna**

KING OF THE TRAP III

By **T.J. Edwards**

GORILLAZ IN THE BAY V

3X KRAZY III

STRAIGHT BEAST MODE III

De'Kari

KINGPIN KILLAZ IV

STREET KINGS III

PAID IN BLOOD III

CARTEL KILLAZ IV

DOPE GODS III

Hood Rich

SINS OF A HUSTLA II

ASAD

YAYO V

Bred In The Game 2

S. Allen

THE STREETS WILL TALK II

By Yolanda Moore

SON OF A DOPE FIEND III

HEAVEN GOT A GHETTO III

SKI MASK MONEY III

By Renta

LOYALTY AIN'T PROMISED III

By Keith Williams

I'M NOTHING WITHOUT HIS LOVE II

SINS OF A THUG II

TO THE THUG I LOVED BEFORE II

IN A HUSTLER I TRUST II

By Monet Dragun

QUIET MONEY IV

EXTENDED CLIP III

THUG LIFE IV

By **Trai'Quan**

Corey Robinson

THE STREETS MADE ME IV
By **Larry D. Wright**
IF YOU CROSS ME ONCE III
ANGEL V
By **Anthony Fields**
THE STREETS WILL NEVER CLOSE IV
By **K'ajji**
HARD AND RUTHLESS III
KILLA KOUNTY IV
By **Khufu**
MONEY GAME III
By **Smoove Dolla**
JACK BOYS VS DOPE BOYS IV
A GANGSTA'S QUR'AN V
COKE GIRLZ II
COKE BOYS II
LIFE OF A SAVAGE V
CHI'RAQ GANGSTAS V
SOSA GANG III
BRONX SAVAGES II
BODYMORE KINGPINS II
By **Romell Tukes**
MURDA WAS THE CASE III
Elijah R. Freeman
AN UNFORESEEN LOVE IV
BABY, I'M WINTERTIME COLD III
By **Meesha**

QUEEN OF THE ZOO III
By **Black Migo**

Protege of a Legend 3

CONFESSIONS OF A JACKBOY III

By Nicholas Lock

KING KILLA II

By Vincent "Vitto" Holloway

BETRAYAL OF A THUG III

By Fre$h

THE MURDER QUEENS III

By Michael Gallon

THE BIRTH OF A GANGSTER III

By Delmont Player

TREAL LOVE II

By Le'Monica Jackson

FOR THE LOVE OF BLOOD III

By Jamel Mitchell

RAN OFF ON DA PLUG II

By Paper Boi Rari

HOOD CONSIGLIERE III

By Keese

PRETTY GIRLS DO NASTY THINGS II

By Nicole Goosby

LOVE IN THE TRENCHES II

By Corey Robinson

IT'S JUST ME AND YOU II

By Ah'Million

FOREVER GANGSTA III

By Adrian Dulan

GORILLAZ IN THE TRENCHES II

By SayNoMore

THE COCAINE PRINCESS VIII

By King Rio

Corey Robinson

CRIME BOSS II

Playa Ray

LOYALTY IS EVERYTHING III

Molotti

HERE TODAY GONE TOMORROW II

By Fly Rock

REAL G'S MOVE IN SILENCE II

By Von Diesel

GRIMEY WAYS IV

By Ray Vinci

<u>**Available Now**</u>

RESTRAINING ORDER **I & II**

By **CA$H & Coffee**

LOVE KNOWS NO BOUNDARIES **I II & III**

By **Coffee**

RAISED AS A GOON I, II, III & IV

BRED BY THE SLUMS I, II, III

BLAST FOR ME I & II

ROTTEN TO THE CORE I II III

A BRONX TALE I, II, III

DUFFLE BAG CARTEL I II III IV V VI

HEARTLESS GOON I II III IV V

A SAVAGE DOPEBOY I II

DRUG LORDS I II III

CUTTHROAT MAFIA I II

KING OF THE TRENCHES

By **Ghost**

LAY IT DOWN **I & II**

LAST OF A DYING BREED I II

BLOOD STAINS OF A SHOTTA I & II III

By **Jamaica**

LOYAL TO THE GAME I II III

LIFE OF SIN I, II III

By **TJ & Jelissa**

BLOODY COMMAS I & II

SKI MASK CARTEL I II & III

KING OF NEW YORK I II,III IV V

RISE TO POWER I II III

COKE KINGS I II III IV V

BORN HEARTLESS I II III IV

KING OF THE TRAP I II

By **T.J. Edwards**

IF LOVING HIM IS WRONG…I & II

LOVE ME EVEN WHEN IT HURTS I II III

By **Jelissa**

WHEN THE STREETS CLAP BACK I & II III

THE HEART OF A SAVAGE I II III IV

MONEY MAFIA I II

LOYAL TO THE SOIL I II III

By **Jibril Williams**

A DISTINGUISHED THUG STOLE MY HEART I II & III

LOVE SHOULDN'T HURT I II III IV

RENEGADE BOYS I II III IV

PAID IN KARMA I II III

Corey Robinson

SAVAGE STORMS I II III
AN UNFORESEEN LOVE I II III
BABY, I'M WINTERTIME COLD I II
By **Meesha**
A GANGSTER'S CODE I &, II III
A GANGSTER'S SYN I II III
THE SAVAGE LIFE I II III
CHAINED TO THE STREETS I II III
BLOOD ON THE MONEY I II III
A GANGSTA'S PAIN I II III
By J-Blunt
PUSH IT TO THE LIMIT
By **Bre' Hayes**
BLOOD OF A BOSS **I, II, III, IV, V**
SHADOWS OF THE GAME
TRAP BASTARD
By **Askari**
THE STREETS BLEED MURDER **I, II & III**
THE HEART OF A GANGSTA I II& III
By **Jerry Jackson**
CUM FOR ME I II III IV V VI VII VIII
An **LDP Erotica Collaboration**
BRIDE OF A HUSTLA **I II & II**
THE FETTI GIRLS **I, II& III**
CORRUPTED BY A GANGSTA I, II III, IV
BLINDED BY HIS LOVE
THE PRICE YOU PAY FOR LOVE I, II ,III
DOPE GIRL MAGIC I II III
By **Destiny Skai**
WHEN A GOOD GIRL GOES BAD

By **Adrienne**
THE COST OF LOYALTY I II III
By Kweli
A GANGSTER'S REVENGE **I II III & IV**
THE BOSS MAN'S DAUGHTERS I II III IV V
A SAVAGE LOVE **I & II**
BAE BELONGS TO ME I II
A HUSTLER'S DECEIT I, II, III
WHAT BAD BITCHES DO I, II, III
SOUL OF A MONSTER I II III
KILL ZONE
A DOPE BOY'S QUEEN I II III
TIL DEATH
By **Aryanna**
A KINGPIN'S AMBITON
A KINGPIN'S AMBITION **II**
I MURDER FOR THE DOUGH
By **Ambitious**
TRUE SAVAGE I II III IV V VI VII
DOPE BOY MAGIC I, II, III
MIDNIGHT CARTEL I II III
CITY OF KINGZ I II
NIGHTMARE ON SILENT AVE
THE PLUG OF LIL MEXICO II
CLASSIC CITY
By **Chris Green**
A DOPEBOY'S PRAYER
By **Eddie "Wolf" Lee**
THE KING CARTEL **I, II & III**
By **Frank Gresham**

Corey Robinson

THESE NIGGAS AIN'T LOYAL **I, II & III**
By **Nikki Tee**
GANGSTA SHYT **I II &III**
By **CATO**
THE ULTIMATE BETRAYAL
By **Phoenix**
BOSS'N UP **I , II & III**
By **Royal Nicole**
I LOVE YOU TO DEATH
By **Destiny J**
I RIDE FOR MY HITTA
I STILL RIDE FOR MY HITTA
By **Misty Holt**
LOVE & CHASIN' PAPER
By **Qay Crockett**
TO DIE IN VAIN
SINS OF A HUSTLA
By **ASAD**
BROOKLYN HUSTLAZ
By **Boogsy Morina**
BROOKLYN ON LOCK I & II
By **Sonovia**
GANGSTA CITY
By **Teddy Duke**
A DRUG KING AND HIS DIAMOND I & II III
A DOPEMAN'S RICHES
HER MAN, MINE'S TOO I, II
CASH MONEY HO'S
THE WIFEY I USED TO BE I II
PRETTY GIRLS DO NASTY THINGS

By Nicole Goosby

TRAPHOUSE KING **I II & III**

KINGPIN KILLAZ I II III

STREET KINGS I II

PAID IN BLOOD **I II**

CARTEL KILLAZ I II III

DOPE GODS I II

By Hood Rich

LIPSTICK KILLAH **I, II, III**

CRIME OF PASSION I II & III

FRIEND OR FOE I II III

By **Mimi**

STEADY MOBBN' **I, II, III**

THE STREETS STAINED MY SOUL I II III

By **Marcellus Allen**

WHO SHOT YA **I, II, III**

SON OF A DOPE FIEND I II

HEAVEN GOT A GHETTO I II

SKI MASK MONEY I II

Renta

GORILLAZ IN THE BAY **I II III IV**

TEARS OF A GANGSTA I II

3X KRAZY I II

STRAIGHT BEAST MODE I II

DE'KARI

TRIGGADALE I II III

MURDAROBER WAS THE CASE I II

Elijah R. Freeman

GOD BLESS THE TRAPPERS I, II, III

THESE SCANDALOUS STREETS I, II, III

Corey Robinson

FEAR MY GANGSTA I, II, III IV, V

THESE STREETS DON'T LOVE NOBODY I, II

BURY ME A G I, II, III, IV, V

A GANGSTA'S EMPIRE I, II, III, IV

THE DOPEMAN'S BODYGAURD I II

THE REALEST KILLAZ I II III

THE LAST OF THE OGS I II III

Tranay Adams

THE STREETS ARE CALLING

Duquie Wilson

MARRIED TO A BOSS I II III

By Destiny Skai & Chris Green

KINGZ OF THE GAME I II III IV V VI VII

CRIME BOSS

Playa Ray

SLAUGHTER GANG I II III

RUTHLESS HEART I II III

By Willie Slaughter

FUK SHYT

By Blakk Diamond

DON'T F#CK WITH MY HEART I II

By Linnea

ADDICTED TO THE DRAMA I II III

IN THE ARM OF HIS BOSS II

By Jamila

YAYO I II III IV

A SHOOTER'S AMBITION I II

BRED IN THE GAME

By S. Allen

TRAP GOD I II III

RICH $AVAGE I II III

MONEY IN THE GRAVE I II III

By Martell Troublesome Bolden

FOREVER GANGSTA I II

GLOCKS ON SATIN SHEETS I II

By Adrian Dulan

TOE TAGZ I II III IV

LEVELS TO THIS SHYT I II

IT'S JUST ME AND YOU

By Ah'Million

KINGPIN DREAMS I II III

RAN OFF ON DA PLUG

By Paper Boi Rari

CONFESSIONS OF A GANGSTA I II III IV

CONFESSIONS OF A JACKBOY I II

By Nicholas Lock

I'M NOTHING WITHOUT HIS LOVE

SINS OF A THUG

TO THE THUG I LOVED BEFORE

A GANGSTA SAVED XMAS

IN A HUSTLER I TRUST

By Monet Dragun

CAUGHT UP IN THE LIFE I II III

THE STREETS NEVER LET GO I II III

By Robert Baptiste

NEW TO THE GAME I II III

MONEY, MURDER & MEMORIES I II III

By **Malik D. Rice**

LIFE OF A SAVAGE I II III IV

A GANGSTA'S QUR'AN I II III IV

Corey Robinson

MURDA SEASON I II III
GANGLAND CARTEL I II III
CHI'RAQ GANGSTAS I II III IV
KILLERS ON ELM STREET I II III
JACK BOYZ N DA BRONX I II III
A DOPEBOY'S DREAM I II III
JACK BOYS VS DOPE BOYS I II III
COKE GIRLZ
COKE BOYS
SOSA GANG I II
BRONX SAVAGES
BODYMORE KINGPINS
By Romell Tukes
LOYALTY AIN'T PROMISED I II
By Keith Williams
QUIET MONEY I II III
THUG LIFE I II III
EXTENDED CLIP I II
A GANGSTA'S PARADISE
By **Trai'Quan**
THE STREETS MADE ME I II III
By **Larry D. Wright**
THE ULTIMATE SACRIFICE I, II, III, IV, V, VI
KHADIFI
IF YOU CROSS ME ONCE I II
ANGEL I II III IV
IN THE BLINK OF AN EYE
By **Anthony Fields**
THE LIFE OF A HOOD STAR
By Ca$h & Rashia Wilson

Protege of a Legend 3

THE STREETS WILL NEVER CLOSE I II III
By K'ajji
CREAM I II III
THE STREETS WILL TALK
By Yolanda Moore
NIGHTMARES OF A HUSTLA I II III
By King Dream
CONCRETE KILLA I II III
VICIOUS LOYALTY I II III
By Kingpen
HARD AND RUTHLESS I II
MOB TOWN 251
THE BILLIONAIRE BENTLEYS I II III
REAL G'S MOVE IN SILENCE
By Von Diesel
GHOST MOB
Stilloan Robinson
MOB TIES I II III IV V VI
SOUL OF A HUSTLER, HEART OF A KILLER I II
GORILLAZ IN THE TRENCHES
By SayNoMore
BODYMORE MURDERLAND I II III
THE BIRTH OF A GANGSTER I II
By Delmont Player
FOR THE LOVE OF A BOSS
By C. D. Blue
MOBBED UP I II III IV
THE BRICK MAN I II III IV V
THE COCAINE PRINCESS I II III IV V VI VII
By King Rio

Corey Robinson

KILLA KOUNTY I II III IV
By Khufu
MONEY GAME I II
By Smoove Dolla
A GANGSTA'S KARMA I II III
By FLAME
KING OF THE TRENCHES I II III
by **GHOST & TRANAY ADAMS**
QUEEN OF THE ZOO I II
By **Black Migo**
GRIMEY WAYS I II III
By Ray Vinci
XMAS WITH AN ATL SHOOTER
By Ca$h & Destiny Skai
KING KILLA
By Vincent "Vitto" Holloway
BETRAYAL OF A THUG I II
By Fre$h
THE MURDER QUEENS I II
By Michael Gallon
TREAL LOVE
By Le'Monica Jackson
FOR THE LOVE OF BLOOD I II
By Jamel Mitchell
HOOD CONSIGLIERE I II
By Keese
PROTÉGÉ OF A LEGEND I II III
LOVE IN THE TRENCHES
By Corey Robinson
BORN IN THE GRAVE I II III

184

Protege of a Legend 3

By Self Made Tay

MOAN IN MY MOUTH

By XTASY

TORN BETWEEN A GANGSTER AND A GENTLEMAN

By J-BLUNT & Miss Kim

LOYALTY IS EVERYTHING I II

Molotti

HERE TODAY GONE TOMORROW

By Fly Rock

PILLOW PRINCESS

By S. Hawkins

<u>BOOKS BY LDP'S CEO, CA$H</u>

TRUST IN NO MAN

TRUST IN NO MAN 2

TRUST IN NO MAN 3

BONDED BY BLOOD

SHORTY GOT A THUG

THUGS CRY

THUGS CRY 2

THUGS CRY 3

TRUST NO BITCH

TRUST NO BITCH 2

TRUST NO BITCH 3

TIL MY CASKET DROPS

RESTRAINING ORDER

RESTRAINING ORDER 2

IN LOVE WITH A CONVICT

LIFE OF A HOOD STAR

XMAS WITH AN ATL SHOOTER

Protege of a Legend 3

www.ingramcontent.com/pod-product-compliance
Lightning Source LLC
Chambersburg PA
CBHW071211260626
47162CB00004B/1261